The Invader
Force Majeure

By
Douglas Fox

Cover art: Fredrik Öhlander unsplash

Paper ISBN: 978-1-7923-9781-3
eBook ISBN: 978-1-7923-9858-2

BISAC: FIC028090, FIC028130, FIC028070

For Baste

Contents

Chapter One
Disaster

Twelve years. Then a slow death.

"Are you sure your calculations are correct?" Thor Haierdood, Jr., the Director of Engineering, asked Michael, his executive assistant.

"They're accurate. There's a slight uncertainty in the precise trajectory, but I have no doubt at all about the outcome. Right now, the planet we are calling "Invader" is frozen, its atmosphere lying on its surface. Its mass is measured at 9.61 Jupiter masses. As it surfs towards the sun it will become a hot Jupiter and fling this planet out of the solar system and into outer space. We will become another rogue planet just like Invader. We will all freeze to death."

"Well then, Michael, has this been distributed to the news media yet?"

"No, it's based on data from one of our own exo-heliospheric survey spacecraft. Our Orbital Mechanics Department just completed the calculations. We're treating everything as proprietary, company-confidential."

"Good, don't release anything. I have a few ideas and I want to be out in front on this one. Any chance of blasting Invader to a different orbit? It's still a long way out."

Titian Space Systems was the largest aerospace company in the world with most of the government's space contracts. This put Thor and Titian in the perfect position to advance their own agendas.

"Not a chance. *Way* too massive. Even though it's far away and too faint for even the ultra-large telescope array to spot it."

The Milky Way probably has hundreds of billions, and possibly trillions, of rogue planets flying about, not to mention countless brown dwarfs, wandering black holes, neutron stars, magnetars, stray intergalactic asteroids and comets of all sizes, and gravitational disturbances that dislodge barrages of comets sending them inwards.

The orbits of stars around the galactic center vary a great deal, and it is common for stars including our own, to pass close to other stars during their lifetime.

Even in the vastness of intergalactic space, it's a statistical certainty that stable planets are occasionally snuffed out. Would we see a dangerous rogue coming? Maybe, or civilization could just as easily be suddenly wiped off the face of the universe with no warning whatsoever. What of humanity, our culture, our rich history and diversity? Are all of the lives that ever lived, all of our strivings, and our multifaceted history a mere quantum ripple too insignificant to notice?

"Boss, you've been itching to send a colony to another solar system as long as I've known you. You're a regular Buck Rogers. What do you think?"

"Yeah, this gives me as much ammunition as I'll ever have. It's a matter of our survival as a species. After all the trials our species has survived, all of the painful steps to create our advanced culture, how could anyone seriously entertain the idea that we would willingly die out with no trace we ever existed?" Thor had been pitching an interstellar colony to the company and the space agency for years.

"You know perfectly well what they will say. Titian and the Space Agency will tell you it's too expensive, too dangerous and uncertain, and if there's any payoff, it's too far in the future. No profit in it. Same old story."

"Maybe they won't object if Titian puts its own resources into it."

"Why would we? It will cost an order of magnitude more even than the fleets of interstellar micro-probes we've sent to other stars so far, and that was huge. The entire company would have to be refocused."

"I know. Interstellar probes were a hard-sell even for the founder of this company, Warner Titian, because it would be centuries before data starting coming back, so who cares and why pay up? This is different."

"You know what you'll hear. Even though we do have some data now about possible destination planets, it's already stale by the time we get it. And the data is just a sparse snapshot. Things could have changed a great deal by the time we finally get to a planet centuries form now. Not to mention we have no time for any prior terraforming that would be required. They will insist it's too much of a longshot gamble, and they might be right. How can you possibly sell that to Old Man Conway?"

Thor observed. "Wouldn't he want to save his own sorry guts? I'll convince him."

"Are you kidding, he hates the sight of you."

"He knows the company will fall apart without me. And besides, He's toast in 12 years anyway and so are we. What's to lose?"

"Why don't we just hunker down in caves like we did during the super-volcanic period of our history," Michael countered. "Why won't he think that's a safer bet? Haven't you been to any of the cave museums?"

"Sure, and it's about cramped quarters, dim artificial light, huge noisy air filtration systems, hydroponics tanks, recyclers, fusion generators, stinky waste reprocessing, same boring food every day, getting sick from watching the same old movie for the sixth time, never any change of scenery. Would have been a great place to camp out and earn a merit badge when I was a scout, but what kind of life is that? Jail sounds like a step up."

"And you think Conway will buy that pitch?"

"If he doesn't there's the prospect that Titian will no longer exist, so who will he order around? Wouldn't he much rather be the grand poohbah dictator of an entire new planet than the supervisor of an underground septic system?"

"I see. So, with Conway, it's about power, money, and luxury."

"And he can't have any of that in a cave. Caves will die after a while. There will no longer be an atmosphere, the planet's internal heat will fade, there won't be a carbon cycle, and sooner or later, everyone freezes to death."

"If you're convinced he'll go for it, then sell it to Conway. If he falls for it, which I doubt, I work for you and I'll do whatever I can. You know, you're just like your old man." Michael would back up his boss, whatever his decision was, same as always.

"I can sell him on it before anyone outside of Titian finds out and comes up with schemes of their own. It should be a few years before the ultra-large telescope array sees Invader, and it becomes common knowledge."

Thor was a congenial sort, a bit taller than average, overweight with a greying, bushy mustache. His office was rather plain with modular furniture, less than you would expect for someone responsible for a large aerospace company's entire engineering effort. It had a small window facing a garage. At least it had an electronic chalkboard and was large enough for a table and eight chairs, a necessity for small technical and staff meetings.

To Conway, the president and CEO, Thor was a political threat. Conway made sure the plainness of Thor's office was a constant reminder of his place in the company. It sent a message that he would progress no higher than his current position. Conway projected that everyone else was just as much of a political schemer as he was, and so viewed anyone in a director or higher position as a threat, regardless of their intentions.

For Thor, however, his position precisely fitted his talents. It was exactly what he wanted. He was in charge of engineering for a company at the forefront of technology and found it quite challenging and satisfying. Thor's father had been a professional explorer and photographer. His pictures appeared all over the internet and on TV, and he had gained a certain notoriety. His father always told Thor to seek and explore as well, because it was his destiny make important new discoveries. Thor internalized some of that fever from his now deceased father and it was expressed in his work. Thor tried to be satisfied and fulfilled with his position, and convinced himself his ambitions were satisfied.

The next day, Michael caught up with Thor. "Well, what did the old man say?"

"Not only did he buy it, he is enthusiastic as long as he goes on the mission, is in charge of everything, runs the whole show, and becomes ruler of the new planet. He wants absolute authority there.

And, he thinks the colony should expand to as many additional planets as possible, all under his dictatorial sway of course."

"And what did you say to that?"

"Yes, of course, since he hasn't got a clue what he's getting into. He thinks he will hop in a capsule, eat a few space meals, and hop out as Grand Poohbah and Exalted Dictator of Galactic New Utopia."

"Ha, even I know better. We can barely engineer enough energy to get our interstellar micro-probes to other star systems in a practical amount of time for future generations to receive the results. Generations elapse before we know anything. Our great-grandchildren are the only ones around when the probes finally arrive at their destinations and send back their discoveries.

"Do you propose sending embryos with minimal support systems, or maybe people in suspended animation in cryogenic modules with more elaborate monitoring and life support, or maybe both?"

"Too early to tell which, but Conway doesn't know we'll freeze his butt. As much energy as possible has to go into propulsion and magnetic radiation shields, and as little as possible into habitat," Thor laughed.

"You know the success rate with cryogenics? It's only 75%. A quarter of them die when they're resuscitated and thawed out. Not to mention that slowing their biological processes and putting them into hibernation in the first place is tricky, too."

"I know that, but so far, they're all terminally ill patients hoping they can wake up to a cure. We'll send healthy specimens. We're zeroing in on better ways to get them to sleep. We've had great luck inducing deep sleep with National Samurai Gladiator re-runs."

Annie Kolar from Sales and Marketing wandered in to interrupt, on an impulse. She was thirtyish, noticeably taller than average, ordinary looks, short dark hair, and dark eyes. She commanded any room she entered just on the basis of her assertiveness. Annie was possessed by whatever urges, emotions, or desires occupied her mind at any particular point in time. Such urges usually hung on to her consciousness for a while, even to the point of obsession, before they were superseded by something else. There was no distinction between wants and needs for her, and she would never lower herself to make such a distinction. Annie acted in the moment. She lived in the here and now. Consistency was a distant planet for her. Dedication and discipline were moons circling that planet. Annie had an unconscious knack for sensing others' vulnerabilities and turning them to her advantage. In short, she was a saleswoman extraordinaire, the best at Titian, and she had the boss's full attention as a result.

"So, what are Curly and Moe hatching up now? You have anything going up in space I can sell? I need commissions. I'm broke again," Annie probed, always a thorn in everyone's side.

"Just business as usual. Throwing some thoughts around," Michael said, trying to put her off.

"Yeah, sure. You never tell the truth, you're both a couple of liars. Tell me what you are planning. I won't leave until I find out."

"All right, we're just throwing out some ideas for a future manned mission. Nothing concrete." Michael was getting annoyed. He would be quite happy if he never saw or heard from Annie again ever.

"Lying again, can't help yourself. Just sitting on your butt all day flapping your jaws as usual. Must be nice. You better tell me what this is about. This is a for-profit company, so I can sell transponders to AI news generators, or rocket seats to wanna-be astronauts. I can even sell these space monkeys training and get double commissions. Thor, you better include me in on whatever it is the two of you are hatching, or you'll both regret it big time. And I want to hear it from you directly, not from your second banana here."

"Sure you will, but if there *is* a mission, we'll pick the crew ourselves. It won't be up to you to decide who goes."

"What kind of attitude is that? You're not a team player. You should be company men. Your attitude sucks. You suck. If you don't play ball with me, I'll tell Conway what you're doing. You are just a couple of lowlifes and the boss should know about it."

"Maybe, just maybe, we do have a new mission in mind for you. Conway will want a crew full of suck-ups and butt kissers. Can you find some?" Michael teased.

"You're just playing with me. Conway will hear about what you said. Michael, you're history around here if I have anything to say about it. There's a commission to be made on every project and I'm going to hound you until I get mine. I'm going up to speak to the boss right now!" Annie raised her voice even higher as she stormed out.

"You're right, Michael. If Conway picks the crew, they will all arrive at the new planet with noses smelling like the boss's posterior, even the embryos. Every decision will be based on politics, not survival. It would be a disaster. We can't let that happen."

"You know as well as I do the success of the mission hangs on the quality, expertise, and spirit of the astronauts as well as on our planning and preparation."

"We'll select who goes, but we have to fake their backgrounds so they all look like yes-men, and coach them on what to say to the boss," Thor replied.

"What kind of instructions did Conway give you anyway?"

"He wants regular briefings. He wants to make the major decisions himself. I'll just tell him what he wants to hear. I can always resort to feeding him a bunch of complicated technical mumbo jumbo like I do sometimes. His ego won't allow him to admit he doesn't have a clue what I'm talking about, and he'll just say 'go ahead but keep me informed.' If he makes a decision I can't live with, I'll do what I have to and try not to be too obvious about it."

"You want Conway to obsess on becoming El Supremo of the Entire Visible Universe and Beyond so he'll totally commit to the project? Sooner or later when any kind of snag develops, he'll panic and reach down to get his hands on the work, then the you-know-what will hit the fan," Michael worried.

"Yeah. I don't have a strategy to deal with that right now. One step at a time," Thor replied.

Michael interjected, "There's something else that bothers me. As soon as an astronaut steps into the cryogenic module, he could be breathing his last. He may not come out of hibernation alive, or he might get irradiated to death on the long journey, or the new planet could be poisonous. It's all very risky. Why would anyone ever want to volunteer for this mission in the first place?"

Thor was optimistic. "We're sure of at least one volunteer already. Annie Kolar has a husband."

"Why don't we just send embryos and some robots to raise and educate them?"

"Annie was raised by a nanny bot and look what happened to her. It takes people with experience and expertise to both explore unknown places and raise embryos. Robots won't be adequate. We have to send both."

Right away, it was time for the overall strategy and planning to commence. There was no time to waste. Critical decisions had to be made up front, and Thor and his assistants had to get them right. There would be no time for back-tracking on this project.

Thor had recruited the company's best exobiologist, Peter Skinner, and exogeologist, John Forbes, along with a few other key players, and swore them to secrecy. It was critical to keep knowledge of Invader secret as long as possible, to avoid interference.

Thor had brought Michael along from a previous company. Michael had a solid engineering background and was detail oriented. His biggest strength was a logical, deductive mind. Michael was an ideal assistant. He had few original or creative ideas of his own, but given a direction and some guidelines he ran with it, ferreting out the details like Sherlock Holmes. He consistently followed through on the loose ends, doggedly monitoring each project's progress and problems. Michael's appearance even resembled a fictional Holmes from a movie, minus the pipe and hat. He was trim, with an oval, clean-shaven face, neatly trimmed hair, a piercing gaze, and a normally serious, all business expression. Michael would play a critical role.

Thor's wife Vanessa stopped by his office the next day. Thor insisted she be granted a security clearance and free access to the engineering offices on Titian's huge, sprawling, and old, but reasonably maintained campus.

"Dear, you've been working way too hard lately. It's almost like you're avoiding Hannah and me. What's the matter? Thought I would drop by for a visit and find out first-hand why you're spending so much time here."

"Keep this quiet, don't tell anyone. It's company top secret until word gets out. We're planning a project to send astronauts to another planet."

"I don't want you getting consumed with it. It's a dream of yours, but you aren't your father you know. Please promise me you'll make time for us," she begged.

"Always, hon."

Thor wanted to do both if he could manage it. He would try. The mission would be extremely demanding but nevertheless, it was his first priority. It was the challenge, a culmination for him. He had to prove to himself he was his famous father's equal. "I'm sure you see, Vanessa, this is the most important and exciting thing any civilization can ever do, perpetuating itself and expanding galaxy-wide."

"Dear, what difference does it make what your culture does and where you live if you don't have close personal relationships? It's the closeness that makes life more than just animal drudgery," raising her voice just a bit.

Thor backed off. "Why don't I order the three of us a special dinner tonight?"

Thor admitted to himself he did look forward to seeing his wife and daughter every evening. "Can't wait. See you at home later."

*   *   *

Thor's considerable analytical and managerial talent would now be tested to the limit. He had a working knowledge of the engineering areas under him, although it was impossible to be an expert in everything.

Before he left for the evening, he called Michael to coordinate their activities.

It helped that Thor was usually a congenial and outgoing sort, although he occasionally got upset when his projects were behind, or hit a snag, at which time Thor nearly lost it a few times. He got along well with most of his staff, understood their problems, could usually sense when they hit a wall, or when they were slacking off or had personal issues that prevented them from working effectively, in which case he took immediate action.

The next day Thor was in his office bright and early at 7:00 a.m. as usual, pursuing the feasibility of the mission with Michael, Forbes, and Skinner.

"Gentlemen," Thor declared as he brandished his glass of water, "You are hereby anointed charter members of the Committee for the Relocation of Advanced Populations. Put it on your resume. Because this is all CRAP if we can't find a planet to go to. John, what are we looking for?

Most stars have planets in a dizzying array of forms and compositions, but planets suitable for colonization are quite rare.

Forbes explained, "First of course is the need for a year-round presence of liquid water. We don't have time to terraform any planets. That takes millennia at best. We need similar gravity, atmospheric pressure, and oxygen level to our own, between about 19% and 29%. The target planets have to be extremely similar to our own to begin with. Ready to go right out of the box. 'Some assembly required' won't cut it.

"Second, there has to be a sizable liquid iron core and rotation rate to generate a magnetic field to deflect stellar wind and interstellar charged particles.

Third, there has to be some protection from UV radiation if the star is hot enough to generate a lot of it and also from galactic gamma rays.

"Fourth, there has to be enough tectonic activity to cycle carbon and keep carbon dioxide, methane and other greenhouse gas levels more or less stable. You have to have a certain amount of shake-and-bake. We also don't want excessive climatic variation, though our species has certainly been able to adapt to a fair amount of that.

"Fifth, we have to avoid flare stars and low mass stars prone to large flares, stars leaving the main sequence, unstable or variable stars, stars with dangerous companions, systems with a lot of debris and planetary bombardment, or systems with especially large planets in close-in orbits. Stars in the middle of their life or a bit younger are better because habitability will last longer and young stars can act up. Hot stars have too short a lifetime, but for cool stars, planets have to orbit too close to the star to stay warm and they usually become tidally locked unless they are massive with sufficient atmospheric density and friction prevent it, limiting the complexity of life. Some planets such as massive, ocean-bound Hycean worlds could still be habitable around these smaller stars, but they are not suitable for colonization.

"As you can see, we're looking for Goldilocks."

Forbes was practically a genius, and he was the most knowledgeable exogeologist Thor knew of, but he had some doubts about how dedicated Forbes was to his work. He was a little too much of a wise guy to suit Thor.

Pete Skinner, the senior exobiologist, laid out additional criteria. The target planet or planets should already have at least simple life forms including photosynthesis, and better still, multicellular life forms, to prove it is habitable. It cannot be sterile. There has to be recycling of oxygen, nitrogen, and minerals. The biochemistry has to be compatible. It wasn't possible to know with current resources if there would be poisons or potential parasites everywhere.

Thor summoned Greenshades from the Interstellar Division. He was in charge of processing data from the micro-probes that were sent to other solar systems. He knew which probes Titian had received the data from and which probes were either still in transit or had reached their destination but their transmissions hadn't been received yet. He had the results of wide band spectroscopic measurements, photos taken with a variety of filters and magnifications, temperature readings, inferred densities, radio and other frequency receiver snapshots, reflectivity values and variations, and magnetometer values, and other data that had been received and analyzed so far, including solar radiation spectrum and intensity and other measurements of the parent star.

Everyone agreed that, if at all possible, they had to hedge their bets and try to colonize more than one planet.

Greenshades proposed five or six possible target planets for further consideration. Thor tasked Forbes, Skinner, Michael, and Greenshades to thoroughly study the research and select the best possibilities. A comparison table showing their merits, directions, distances, and the characteristics of their stars would summarize their findings. Selecting targets was the first critical decision. Engineering requirements would follow.

A week later, the so-called Committee for the Relocation of Advanced Populations reconvened in Thor's office.

Forbes reported the results. "We've identified our best target planets, three of them. The best and most likely to support advanced life is thirty-one-point-eight light years away. It's one of only two planets within seventy-five light years we know of that might not require terraforming. The third planet is a hundred and twenty light years away.

"The closest planet has about ten percent less mass and its gravity is only about five percent less than ours. The atmosphere is estimated to be only 80 percent as thick, so living there would be like living at altitude, but it's more towards the inner edge of its star's habitable zone and warmer than our planet. Spectroscopy shows an oxygen concentration of about 22%. That and the trace presence of methane indicates life is present. It has a bit higher density than our planet, meaning probably more metals and a larger iron core, and we can't be sure, but it seems to have a vertical spin axis, so it should have a strong enough magnetic field. There is water vapor in its atmosphere although it's not an ocean world. We can't say for sure, but continents with tectonic activity seem highly probable, we hope enough for effective recycling, but there's no way to tell. Could be lots of water with volcanic islands for all we know. The planet's star is G2, brighter than ours, middle aged, with a higher metallicity, and with a suitable spectrum for photosynthesis, so that fits."

"How reliable is your information?" Thor asked.

"It's not a transiting planet, but it was the target of one of our more primitive first-generation micro-probe clusters, and we have some good information, though not as good as we've gotten from more recent probes. I do have reservations about it. The probes imaged bright points of light from other potential planets in this system, but none of them appear habitable," Forbes replied.

"What about the second target planet?" Thor asked.

"It was the target of a fleet of second-generation micro-probes. It's another thirty-eight light years away and orbits a K3 dwarf star. It doesn't transit and it's too far away for our ground-based telescopes to directly image. Spectroscopic analysis showed it has the right atmospheric composition and calculations indicate it isn't tidally locked. The planet is also near the inner edge of its habitable zone, and as its star brightens over time, the planet will probably overheat in another billion years. That's not something to worry about. As a bonus, there are a couple of additional planets colonists could migrate to from this one, assuming they can be terraformed over time. One of these two other planets orbits a yellow dwarf star in a triple system eight light years away. The other orbits a K4 star that is currently far away, a hundred and two light years, but it will pass through the outer edges of the colony planet's Oort cloud in another two point two million years and be easily accessible then."

"And the third planet?"

"The third and farthest planet orbits a K5 star a hundred and twelve light years away. We also have basic information about it from first-generation micro-probes that survived the trip, but not as much as for the others. Calculations indicate it should also not be tidally locked, but we can't be absolutely certain."

"Out of the billions of stars and planets in our neighborhood of the galaxy there surely must be other possibilities," Thor questioned.

"Absolutely, but we just don't have the data, so we don't know. Fleets of micro-probes have been launched to scores of promising solar systems, but either they haven't arrived yet or else they arrived but their telemetry data has not reached us yet. For example, there is another very promising triple star system thirty-five point seven light years away in the general direction of our primary target. It has G2 and K1 stars with confirmed planets in their habitable zones. That's all we know about this system, but a third-generation micro-probe swarm is on its way, arriving in another 15 years."

"Too late to do us any good."

"Regarding your question, we rule out M stars and fainter K star systems because their rocky planets will be close to the star and tidally locked, and any atmosphere they might have would probably be depleted or stripped away by intense flares from the nearby star. O, B, A, and brighter F stars are too short-lived. Younger stars would not have had time for their planets to evolve suitable conditions for advanced life. It isn't straightforward, but metallicity also influences the size and number of planets a star has. Altogether, more than eighty-five per cent of stars have to be ruled out from having planets suitable for us to colonize. It requires probes to explore the rest before we can know."

Forbes then asked, "What is your reservation about the closest planet?"

"Our micro-probes encountered suspected faint, transient low-frequency radio signals, and the planet was brighter than it should have been at night. That is a possible sign of a rudimentary intelligent life form just entering a technological phase. But that is extremely unlikely. The signals were probably due to extensive lightning storms, or maybe to circuit noise from cosmic ray damage to a probe's radio, or caused by solar activity, by reflections from an undiscovered or volcanically active moon, or by planet-wide storms."

"What do you think is the likelihood there are technological creatures, even if their technology is crude?"

"If there are any, we'd better be the savior and get there before it's too late and they ruin their environment, or they overpopulate and render the planet permanently uninhabitable. Seriously, I think that's extremely unlikely. If we find a race of Godzillas with laser rifles, maybe we should just move on."

That remark was yet another example of why Thor still worried about whether Forbes was serious enough about his job.

They all knew they had to consider every possibility, every contingency, and have a workable plan. Unexpected dangers were no doubt lurking. Their data was sparse and there would be unexpected situations. The nature of life on other planets was unknown. Cataclysmic events could transpire during the centuries between the micro-probe data transmissions and when they arrived at a planet.

Thor noted that the advance probes might give them a heads up on some of this as they approached their destination, if probe sensors were well-designed.

Skinner opined. "Look, we know we will encounter new life forms. It's a requirement. And what will we find? We can make some educated guesses based on the conditions, geography, geology, atmospheric makeup, and chemistry on a planet."

"You know the principle of biology that 'form follows function'. It means that the behavior comes first, then the anatomy evolves to make the behavior more efficient. Life specializes and gets better at it. We have to understand what the living forms on the target planet have to do to survive, how are they compelled to act, so we can anticipate and so that we ourselves can adapt.

"Let me give you an example of 'form follows function'. Our ancestors first started to habitually walk upright, and then after that their feet flattened, hips tilted, knee joint enlarged, face flattened, and so on to make it efficient.

"Some call this compulsive behavior instinctive, some call it archetypal, or both. The archetypes can be exact and specific like with insects. Exact instinctive behavior eliminates the need for intelligence and it makes the organism less adaptable, unless adaptation relies on mutation. General behavior patterns, on the other hand, allow for intelligent choice but also introduce mistakes.

"Archetypes are the very nature of an animal, how it is predestined to act and possibly think. For high intelligence and adaptability, archetypes must be amorphous, generalized behavioral patterns with many nodes. They will not be 'on' all of the time, but will instead be triggered by any situation that resembles the general pattern. And altering a node is tricky. It's highly likely to have repercussions at other nodes. So, maybe we can surmise what some of the archetypes of the new life forms we encounter might be, in order to predict what they will do and how we respond.

"Let me give you a very simple example. Cats can catch and eat snakes. Anything long and thin fits their pattern of a snake. A string, a falling stick, a piece of yarn blowing in the breeze all resemble a snake and they can attack it. Snakes have many appearances. What if the cat attacks a viper or a mamba or a bushmaster or a poison salamander? The pattern is general and the archetype doesn't understand the danger or distinction, so it could be a fatal encounter. Just remember that the more flexible the pattern is, the more scope there is for reason, adaptability, and potential intelligence, but at the same time, the higher the chance of mistakes.

"Beware, because this applies to our artificially intelligent computers, too. They will encounter things they were never trained for. Will they make fatal mistakes like the cat? Maybe they already have. The probes we sent definitely encountered things they were never trained for. In the end, they also must use patterned interpretation and reasoning. Have they already fatally misled us about what they found at our target planets? Is the data they send us trustworthy?"

Forbes responded, "What if plants or animals on our new planet are highly destructive, fatally dangerous, destined to ruin their planet? Should we play God and design and unleash a virus to genetically alter their predisposition? Should we have a contingency plan for that? Is it ethical?"

Thor replied, "We can think about it. Personally, I don't see anything wrong with saving other lifeforms from themselves. Would you cancel the mission then?"

Forbes smart answer, "You can cancel it if you want, but I for one don't intend to hang around here and freeze to death."

Chapter Two
Not Business as Usual

"There's no longer much question. I have an inside informant at Titian who told me they think that a large rogue planet they are calling 'Invader' will surf through the inner solar system in a dozen years or so, and it will fling this planet out into space and eternal oblivion. They've known this for a while now and they are already planning for it. It's strictly hush-hush, and I am sworn to secrecy, but we need a plan. We need to be ahead of the crowd, so what will we do?" Howard Blaine, founder, president, and CEO of Howard Blaine Industries was in his office with his son, the senior vice president.

Blaine Industries had manufacturing plants scattered all over. The original and largest plant, along with company headquarters, was located in a formerly run down decaying northern city. Howard Blaine considered it a public service to renovate the now-prosperous area. His office was a modest corner affair with comfortably worn furniture, suitable for what he needed to do. His son Brandon's office was equal in size to Howard's and located next to it. They shared a private bathroom, kitchen, and executive conference room. Each had a fold-out couch in case they worked into the night.

Brandon responded, "Looks like we have an unavoidable and unpleasant future to prepare for. What do *you* suggest?"

"I don't care to be interstellar toast, along with you and everyone we care about. There's no choice but to refocus the company."

Brandon piped up, "We should build a cave ecosystem and live there."

The two Blaines were experienced cavers and enjoyed the advantages of living underground, the even climate, the privacy, the freedom of design and not having to adhere to rectangular forms, the simplicity of adding living space when they wanted to. There were places on the planet where, like the Blaines, people had fixed up and furnished old mines and caves, even making them luxurious to live in.

There were also people who still lived in caves on remote islands much like their ancestors. The Blaines' own underground getaway seemed natural by now.

"It will be a huge effort. Making it self-contained, sustainable, and maintainable, maybe for centuries. I'd like you to take the first cut at a plan, and don't tell anyone," Howard said.

"OK. It's more likely to be successful if we minimize the scale and the risks. Easier to disguise what we're doing and keep it secret. Our cave only has to be big enough for ourselves, our extended family, skilled workmen, medical staff, and the like. And it has to be defendable. We both know that when the end is near and word gets out, the masses will show up with shovels, guns, and dynamite."

"What do I always tell you, Brandon? Think big! Let's save as many people as we can.

"When you start your plan, determine what talents and systems it will take. Identify the best talent available to us. Locate the equipment and supplies we can supply ourselves and what we have to procure. We are lucky we manufacture things people need, like cold fusion and geothermal power sources, winter clothes, and more, and in quantities well beyond our own needs. What we can't use in a cave, we can sell, trade, or even give away."

Howard Blaine was energized. While Howard Blaine was troubled by the depravation and suffering that was to come, building his business empire had given way to the tedium of maintaining it. Now he felt a new and overwhelming sense of purpose again.

Brandon was wiggling and becoming uncomfortable. "What if we try to do too much? There's a lot more risk to it. Too many people to spill the beans. We could fall short on supplies, resources, and equipment. More systems prone to failure. Harder to maintain air seals and oxygen and warmth. And we only have one shot at this. None of us will survive if we screw it up."

Brandon's face was starting to turn red. He was noticeably uncomfortable. He idolized his father and seldom summoned the courage to disagree.

"Brandon, I want you to expand your comfort zone. How do you think Blaine Industries grew so large? Thorough planning is the key. The backup plan can include a smaller cave. Personally, if we could have saved thousands but didn't make the effort, my conscience will torment me the rest of my days. I hope yours would, too. Can I count on you?"

"You know you can, Dad. Maybe start a plan for both a large cave and a smaller one."

"A larger cave system might divert attention from a smaller private one."

"I want to plan for psychological screening, too," Brandon added. "How many people want to be buried alive and spend their lives entombed with no sunlight, no scenery, stuck with nowhere to go and no new horizons to explore? Remember what happened last time we took some newbies with us to the Redstone Cave? They panicked and that was just a day trip."

"Yeah, there's a lesson there," Howard added.

They had to plan a cave system that was complete, entirely self-contained, maintainable for millennia including the power sources, with everything as recyclable as possible, and with all essential human needs met. After a while, there would be no life and nothing they could extract or use from the frozen surface.

The overall plan was first, then they had to nail down the details, sequences of events, dependencies, and materials. They had to be systematic so they didn't miss anything. Necessary jobs to build and maintain the cave system had to be enumerated, along with the skill set for each. Once that was accomplished, they could start to identify and recruit the best talent for each job at each stage. Then there were the robots and spare parts they would need, above and below ground.

They knew they would have to offer a place in the caves for their workers. They also had to acquire all of the materials and other resources they needed up front, as soon as possible. In a few years, there would be heavy competition for food, power sources, and other necessities. They decided it was least risky to plan a large-sized habitat first with the possibility of scaling it down.

One example stood out in their minds.

It was almost a disaster when they took Leroy Collins and his wife and brother caving at Redstone, and it wasn't the first time something like that had happened. The usual dangers were getting wedged into a tight space, getting a limb caught, being closed off or buried by falling rocks, steep climbs, mud, water hazards, sudden flooding, and the difficulty of rescue.

He crawled in first with Brandon taking up the rear following the brother and Leroy. No sooner were they all into the neck past the sunlight of the entrance than Leroy's wife started shaking with fear, immobilized, dizzy and disoriented, turning red, and with her breathing becoming rapid and shallow. She kept repeating, "I can't do it, I can't move!" The wife was immobilized with fear and there was nothing Howard could do. Brandon and the brother backed out. They asked Leroy to try to calm his wife and induce her to wiggle back out to no avail. Finally, Leroy managed to pull her back, inch by inch.

After cleaning a few of her scratches the men went back to the narrow crawl behind a waiting Howard. No sooner had the brother gotten to the end of the neck when he became claustrophobic repeating, "I can't breathe, it's too tight, I have to get out of here. Back he went. Once in the first cavern Howard, Brandon, and Leroy were confronted by the irritating and persistent musty odor of bat droppings, squinting in the dim lighting from their headlamps. Howard and Brandon no longer noticed such things. Leroy became irritable and stated, "This is not for me." That was the end of the day's caving adventure.

So, the psychological aspects of living in a confined space would be unbearable for some. How much worse might it be when hundreds or thousands of people are trapped and crowded together underground, with little privacy, never able to emerge into the light of day? When would it start to feel like being buried in a tomb? How many people would go insane? Some people would be unable to adapt and would have to be turned away.

Howard took care to select an easy cave with a narrow but mostly level neck of an entrance opening up into a cavern. It was defendable and not far from one of their offices. Best of all, they had already purchased the property the previous year.

Brandon formed a group to help draft the plan. He included a biologist, an ecologist, mining, computer, electrical, and mechanical engineers, an AI/robotics expert, and a security expert. He limited the committee to around a dozen members to keep it productive.

They had to identify anything that could be automated or that they could use robots to do.

Everyone expected that as the reality of Invader set in, people wouldn't see a point to working any more. Labor was sure to become a scarce commodity.

Some people would become lawless and ask themselves, what can the authorities do to them? Life is ending anyway. Plenty of desperate people with nothing to lose. Many people would abandon self-control and act out. Security would become paramount.

A ninety-hour week was coming up for the committee.

Brandon asked, "What will happen to the business, Dad? It will cease to exist in twelve years. Credit availability will end, nobody will work anymore, markets will dry up, raw materials will disappear."

"I'm putting Tim in charge of corporate planning while we concentrate on habitat. He will be sworn to secrecy until our fate leaks out. Have Judy call him in here now."

Howard Blaine was a very controlled, logical, dedicated, purposeful individual guided by strong moral principles. His thought was logical, step-by-step, calculating, and meticulous. His emotions were well-suppressed and controlled, though Howard was compassionate in his unrecognized and unexpressed core. That meant the decisions he would have to make troubled him even more. He tended to keep his plans to himself, sharing his thoughts with his son and others only after they were well-developed in his own mind.

Blaine had amassed billions. In spite of that, he led a modest life style, not at all lavish. He specialized in the manufacture of necessities, things people and especially businesses had to buy. This also satisfied his subconscious tendencies, because he felt he was fulfilling others' needs through his work. Not to mentioned it put his company in a good position to supply the future caves.

Brandon was always close to his father; after his mother died when Brandon was three years old, they were even closer. Brandon strove to emulate his father. As a result, his individual tendencies and latent talents were suppressed, but it hadn't seemed to matter until now. Brandon found his life to be very satisfying on many levels. Now, however, Brandon's individual tendencies were starting to come to the fore, forcing him to break away from his father to find his own life. It would be a difficult and scary time. It was something he was quite unprepared for. For the time being, Brandon was still in his comfort zone, but that wouldn't last much longer. The main difference between the two was that, unlike his father, Brandon tended to be more gregarious, outgoing, and conservative.

Vice President for operations Timothy Chandler entered Howard's office.

Blaine laid out his plan for the business. "Tim, we are refocusing this business. Brandon briefed you about Invader and swore you to secrecy. We will create a self-sustaining underground habitat that will last many millennia, and that is now our primary focus. Manufacturing necessities people will need is our next priority. All other lines of business should be phased out. I'm counting on you to come up with a plan as soon as possible.

"What are my guidelines?"

"Work with Brandon. Come up with lists of supplies, equipment, things we need. See what we can convert and manufacture ourselves. The more self-reliant we are, the sooner we will succeed and we won't need to compete for resources if we can produce them ourselves. Any machinery, robots, inventory, anything that can be modified for use underground, come up with a conversion plan. Scavenge anything you can. Sell off everything else while there is still a market for it, and use the proceeds to buy things we can't produce. Phase out auto accessories, summer and fashion clothes and accessories, jewelry, appliances like air conditioners and lawn mowers, cosmetics, and any other product line that won't be a future necessity.

Convert warehouses to stockpile things we will need ourselves. And don't neglect security. Talk to Julia in Marketing. We need an idea of what will sell in the future and what won't, given the circumstances, so that means a new marketing plan. Julia should get your inputs as a basis for her new plan.

"Assume a developing labor shortage and automate everything you can. Both of you keep me posted daily if any problems arise. This is your top priority. Delegate everything else. And Tim, keep this quiet. Let people assume you are off your rocker if they want to. Throw them off with some wild story if they question you."

Howard Blaine's decisiveness was one of the keys to his success. Still, there were important unknowns to ponder. When would shortages arise and which items would be hardest to get? When would law and order break down? When would official corruption become the norm and when would the inevitable government confiscations, price controls, and anti-hoarding laws start? Would there be new regulatory roadblocks? How would Blaine protect his factories and his caves and hide the supplies?

The first big roadblock was soon apparent. Brandon reported, "We're ready to start some of the construction inside our main cave, but we don't have permits for any of it even though we bought this particular property a year ago. That will delay us by months or years. They want public hearings, environmental impact reports, community feedback, water resource studies, you name it."

"Brandon, you're well aware we can't afford to waste time on pointless government red tape. Put someone on permits. Bribe the people you can, get some of our legal staff to tie them up, whatever it takes, but we proceed immediately no matter what roadblocks the government throws in our way. I have no patience for this kind of nonsense.

"The time will come when people can't deny what is about to happen. They won't worry about consequences and neither will we, so proceed with the construction. I never thought it would come to this, but bribery and blackmail will save lives. Goods, not money, will become the currency of bribes. Find a secret stash for groceries and wine. And I'm sure my corporate jet can be put to good use for fact finding junkets to suppliers and refuges around the world."

Brandon's focus included finding strategic allies; identifying key subcontractors; directing the legal department to find ways around regulatory and other hangups; courting targeted legislators, regulators, and other officials; creating a slush fund for payoffs; pursuing strategic resource and property acquisitions; ordering a fleet of the newest feature rich SF10 security robots; and 1001 other tasks.

But Blaine Industries wasn't alone in starting an effort to build underground habitats. Jeffrey Hughes, great grandson of the founder of Hughes Undersea Resources, already had an ongoing contract to design an underground habitat intended as a base for one of the atmosphere-free moons in the solar system. He already constructed some test caves and had amassed valuable knowledge that would be useful. On the advice of his father, Brandon contacted Hughes, pretending that he was interested in constructing his own private luxurious family cave, and could they pool their expertise? And in the interests of family privacy, would Hughes please keep this confidential? After all, Brandon claimed, the wealthy had their private bunkers, and the Blaines wanted a state-of-the-art underground bunker. At least, that was the cover story Brandon and his father decided upon.

Additional competition was sure to spring up. United Igloo LLP for one was certain to have an idea or two.

There were a lot of engineering and strategic details, some of which Hughes already had experience with. For example, how to mine frozen surface oxygen and dispose of waste carbon dioxide, how to stage independent backup systems, and other Hughes expertise would be most useful.

They had to plan, obtain, hide, and preserve food stockpiles needed in the cave until the underground biospheres were productive.

History demonstrated that in the event of food shortages, the government would seize all farm output and food warehouse contents and put them in their own stockpiles. The politically connected would eat first, and good luck to the rest.

A week later Brandon again reported to his father, accompanied by Chandler. "It's feasible to design and build for five up to ten or twelve thousand. We will give you a firm number when we are further along."

"You know, somebody has to decide who gets in and who is excluded. Stockpiling now means withholding food from people during the months before Invader arrives when it's scarce. Someone has to play God. How can any one of us decide with a clear conscience?" Chandler asked.

"I don't intend to play god," Howard Blaine stated.

"You may not have any choice," Chandler replied.

"You know what bothers me more? People will be clamoring for the government to save them. They know that governments around the world build underground bunkers for anywhere from three hundred high ranking officials to three-hundred thousand military personnel, though they aren't necessarily biospheres and they're intended to be temporary shelters. If they figure out we have stockpiles, they'll send an army to take them from us. How can we keep our plans quiet?"

More staff entered as Chandler left.

"Let me introduce two of our economists, Dr. Paul Smith and Dr. Alan Jones. They made a few predictions."

Smith responded, "To summarize, first and foremost, as the reality of this disaster starts to sink in, people will lose their sense of future and purpose, their motivations will wane, and there will be extreme changes to our society. Many will remain in denial, but they will finally be forced to react to the changes around them. Studies show that when enough people, say ten percent, adopt the new meme and realize that most of them will be left to freeze in the cold, desperation, mob psychology, and lawlessness will take over. Nobody can predict exactly when or how things will play out. Nor have we heard of any social psychologist with a track record who can predict what mobs will do. My guess is that prosperous and influential people and organizations who benefit from the system will downplay the danger and draw out the timeline, so they can hang onto the status quo as long as possible. Eventually, though, economy will break down and make it impossible to work and get materials."

"What else?"

"Students at all levels will drop out of schools when they realize there is no future and education won't help them. There will be exceptions who value learning, but there will also be a lot of professors out of work. Some of them might have talent and expertise we can use."

"And then?"

"Since there will no longer be career paths or any reason to pursue one, and no incentive to save or build for the future, work hours and productivity will plunge. Savings will be spent and prices will soar. Towards the end, food will become the new currency. Powerful forces, including dictators, governments, and special interests, will want to own and control that currency.

"YOLO will reign supreme. People and companies will try to borrow as much as they can but there will be no credit available for them or us except at ruinous short-term rates. The government will respond to the crunch same as they have in the past, by 'printing' ever increasing amounts of money for loans, inflating the currency until it is worthless. Barter and goods will be the name of the game for us and for everybody."

Blaine concluded, "We intend to borrow and spend all the money we can lay our hands on right now, and start building our non-perishable inventory. Pay it all back in cheap money later or never. What else?"

"A big demand will build for both luxuries and necessities, but for other non-essentials demand will stagnate or drop. Demand will rise for luxury housing, but mortgage loans will dry up. We need to focus our business lines accordingly.

"Besides all that, I expect a lot of inertia at first, business as usual and a preoccupation with personal matters. Most of the public will remain focused on the name of the next Royal baby. At first, they will pay scant attention to the bigger picture. That will give us small window to act, so we should take advantage of it, because things will become chaotic, difficult, and unpredictable few years from now."

"Thank you. Anything else for the business plan?"

"In the end, there will be lots of people who don't want to leave their home or neighborhood. They will stay there stockpiling fuel and supplies, not willing to face the fact that it won't help them. Mobs and gangs will rule the planet. People and their supplies won't be safe and neither will we.

"Everyone knows mob behavior is fickle and can jump unpredictably from one demagogue to another, but at some point, we will all be subject to mob rule. A low profile will be the best defense.

"As for the government, tax revenues will drop drastically. Governments' demands on the people will rise geometrically at the same time peoples' willingness to pay higher taxes drops precipitously. The government will no longer be able to borrow, either, since everyone knows they never pay back what they owe, so it's another incentive for them to print like mad and make things a lot worse. The government contracts to build and maintain most of our infrastructure for us. As tax revenues plunge, maintenance will suffer. Roads, airports, navigation systems, policing, and other essential services will all start to crumble. The importance of this last item is that personal safety and property rights, the most legitimate policing function, will fail. In the end, the government won't have spendable money and it will simply confiscate whatever it wants at the point of a gun, claiming eminent domain.

"Utilities and infrastructure will be subject to vandalism and theft, and will no longer be maintained. We will need to build and maintain our own company infrastructure like water and waste facilities and a private fleet of armored trucks with security."

"Thank you, I think. That's a lot to ponder and include in the business plan."

A few days later Howard told Brandon, "I want you to entice Thor Haierdood, the chief engineer from Titian Space Systems, to join our team. As everyone knows, they build space stations and capsules, planetary shelters, and the like, with self-contained environmental systems. He could be a valuable addition."

"Dad, pardon me, but I thought Thor was a screw-up and Conway was the brains of that operation."

"That's what Conway tells everyone who will listen, but I have it from inside sources that it's quite the opposite. Without Thor, their best talent would leave and the whole place would implode. Staff loyalties are to Thor, not the organization. See if you get him. We pay top dollar, top benefits, stock options, whatever he wants."

"I'll pull out all the stops."

"I'm telling you, Mr. Conway, Thor and Michael are plotting something against you. You'd better find out what it is and put a stop to it. And you should hear what they said about you yesterday." Annie had a bargaining chip and she intended to use it.

Bernie M. Conway secretly craved power and control. Actually, it was a secret only to him while it was blatantly obvious to everyone else. His talents were mainly political. The many other skills and abilities he attributed to himself were mostly imaginary. He assumed that anyone around him with any sort of special knowledge, skill, or ambition was a direct threat. He felt no choice but to neutralize all of these supposed threats at every opportunity.

Conway occupied an obscenely spacious, outlandishly furnished corner suite with the best view on the main Titian campus. Besides an enormous plush inner office, his suite included a private bathroom, kitchen, conference room, dressing room, gym, and bedroom furnished in antiques. His penthouse office had a large picture window with a view of the ocean.

Conway corrected Annie, "For your information, Titian will be the chief contractor on a mission to a new planet. I will be the commander of the mission, and I will be the president, CEO, and autocrat of the planet. And this is strictly hush-hush, nobody knows, so if you spill a word of it, you're fired and black-listed. Play ball and you could become filthy rich."

"You're crazy. What makes you think you will even survive such a risky space mission? It's just plain dangerous. Your big fat enormous plush desk chair won't even fit in a space capsule. You run a huge company and have a great influence over the government. You get whatever you want. Who can stop you? That's my philosophy. It's every man for himself, just like always. Why gamble on some lark that can get you killed when you have a sure thing here and now?"

"Always the pessimist. I want absolute, unlimited authority. I want everything done my way and that's what I'll get. Can you imagine running an entire planet? And by the way, this is still a profit-making company and I'm counting on you to keep the money rolling in. Shouldn't you be at your desk?"

Annie countered, "What are you talking about? Do you have inside information about a nuclear war and you're planning an escape? Is it a doomsday bomb? I know you always have inside information. Do you know something is about to happen?"

"What if I did? Why would I tell the likes of you?"

"We both know government money is the lifeblood of this operation, and most of our revenues come from the public sector. What do you think will happen when the public finally realizes there's a bigger reality show going on outside the internet? What happens when they find out a nuclear war is coming their way? They will demand that the government save them. Our funding will get cut."

"Don't shortchange me. I have a lot more leverage than you think I do. The government will turn to us for what I tell them they need."

"All I can say is, if there's a catastrophe, better grab everything you can as fast as you can right now and then live out the rest of your time in obscene opulence and total luxury."

"Of course, you are exactly right. If the public senses an emergency they will demand to be saved. And demagogues everywhere will rush in to promise them what they want, in exchange for power and money, of course. Including Titian. We will offer a crash program to save the world. The public will demand to be saved, cost be damned, and I can become the savior. Is that what you're thinking? If I play my cards right, the money would pour in faster than you can say Swiss bank account. Is your little brain following me on this? Don't be so small-minded. If you behave, maybe I'll cut you in on some of the action."

"What does it matter, anyway? You're too cheap to ever pay me a decent commission on anything."

"You already have the highest commission schedule in the company."

"Liar. I guess there's no stopping you now, is there? Should I call you 'majesty'?"

"You're missing the entire point and here's an example. In times of crisis, people like Reverend Franklin use every channel at his disposal to talk about purifying souls before it's too late. Franklin has a lot of followers you know. He needs to be neutralized. What do you suppose will happen when he convinces our employees to quit and the taxpayers to leave and go up on the mountaintop with him to wait for deliverance?"

Annie was sure this couldn't work. "Who will follow him? He's just a crank and so are you." Being the top salesperson in the company, Annie was the only one who could get away with talking to Conway in this manner, and she knew it.

"I, I mean Titian, will be the greater savior. Look, if you found a way to rule the world, have anything you ever wanted just by commanding it, wouldn't *you* do it? Of course you would. That's exactly what you were talking about."

"I wish I did know what you're babbling about."

"Sorry to stop you, but right now, I have a space mission to carry out, not to mention a golf date with the Secretary of Defense, and I don't want to keep her waiting. If you are so intent on grabbing all the money you can lay your hands on, why don't you go back to your desk and sell something. Maybe we can work out a new commission schedule."

"No, you won't do that, I know you." Annie was really mad by now. She walked out fuming."

*　　*　　*

Titian had the contract to monitor and maintain their fleet of exo-heliospheric survey spacecraft. In order to buy time after discovering Invader, they secretly commanded a coding change to disguise the critical data and replay previously recorded telemetry. The spacecraft would be reprogrammed to divert their gaze away from Invader before restoring live telemetry.

Eventually, Invader would become just visible to the ultra-large telescope array as a faint smudge of light. When the government figured out what was unfolding, it would be in their interest to avoid starting a panic, so everything would be classified top secret. Anyone who suspected anything would be labelled a kook and a fool, and reminded that there are no UFOs, either.

"What do you know about a planet or planets called 'Nibiru' or 'Invader'?" the Secretary quizzed Conrad. "Our phone taps picked up some chatter about a collision with a giant planet. Is there a threat?"

It was time for a calculating Conway to start his grand lobbying campaign. "Ms. Secretary, we are looking at telemetry from our spacecraft for hints. As far as I know, there's nothing to worry about, but what if? I will summon my engineers and find out what is going on."

Of course, Conrad had known for many months what was going on, but wanted to keep the government dependent on Titian and off his back as long as possible. "Ms. Secretary, you could end up in a bind. If there is a threat, you don't want to confirm and release that information because it will start an escalating panic. On the other hand, you want the government to appear to be on top of the situation, be proactive, and have a plan, when the public finds out. Your timing has to be impeccable. You have to be ahead of the rumor but not too early or too late. You can play the hero or the fool, be the savior or get fired, so be careful."

"Need I remind you whatever information you have is top secret? And I expect to be the first to know. I will be the conduit to the Prime Minister."

"Of course."

"Do I have your word Titian will share any new knowledge of the situation with me first? I will be your sole point of contact?"

"Certainly." (Can you swing a golf club with your fingers crossed?).

*   *   *

Page 35

A year later, the jig was finally up. The government's ultra-large telescope array spotted barely visible Invader in the Oort cloud and determined that it was potentially on a path towards the inner solar system. Thor informed Conway the path was becoming obvious, so Conway called the Defense Secretary with the news. Of course, Titian had used its spacecraft from the beginning to secretly map the planet's precise path.

So, Conway got a call from the Prime Minister himself. The Vice Chancellor contacted him first: "Mr. Conway, the Prime Minister would like to speak with you…"

"Yes, Mr. Prime Minister. I understand that. We have been on top of it since we notified the Secretary. What I propose is a crash program. Prepare a mission to send a series of hydrogen bombs to the planet to nudge it off course, then blow it up. You know this company is in a unique position to mount that kind of elaborate operation. We could have everything ready for a launch in, say, about a year. I suggest a secret program using some defense or spy agency slush fund. When the rockets are well underway, let me suggest you can then tell the public there was a threat and you have neutralized it. No worries. You are the hero."

After another pause, "Yes, Mr. Prime Minister. I will have an estimate for you by the end of the week. Goodbye, sir."

Conway couldn't help laughing. You can't nudge a super-Jupiter with hydrogen bombs. The only chance was to nudge some very large asteroid onto a collision course with it, but there were no candidates. The fool will fall on his face; he would embarrass himself in front of the entire world. When he did, Conway would call a press conference and say to the world, "I told the Prime Minister he was making a mistake, his idea wouldn't work. He just wouldn't listen. I'm a patriot. I had to do as the Prime Minister commanded and go forward with the project. We gave it our best effort. Now let me tell you what he should have done…" The prestige, power, and money Conway craved would come his way if he gave a good performance, if only for a few years.

The cost Conway proposed would be obscene. There would be some bargaining but how could the Prime Minister possibly say no? He was trapped.

It was now time to lobby for the project. Conway ordered his secretary, "Get me Gleason at the Space Agency, set up a call with Senator Picador from the defense committee, and get a hold of my chief lobbyist."

Conway's secretary overheard him on his phone. "Remember, Senator, your daughter-in-law is making six figures with Titian as an executive receptionist. I'm sure you can see the necessity for this project…"

Next, Conway ordered his secretary to connect him with Barrow, Chairman of the Board of Titian.

Conway either had the dirt on, or a strategic understanding with, every member of the Board of Directors. The Directors he couldn't control had long since been replaced with ones he could.

He expected the Board to compensate him not only for his current post, but for his anticipated future triumphs. He made certain he got huge bonuses on every possible pretext, regular large raises, stock options, and stock distributions.

"Barrow, I want your full support on two upcoming projects. You've heard about Invader. The government found out now, but it's still hush-hush. The Prime Minister wants a mission to divert the damn thing with hydrogen bombs using our rockets. It will be a fat sole source contract with obscene profits. I also need to replenish my research fund to send some very elaborate probes to three planets. Will you support me on this and help convince the other board members? There will be some fat contracts for your other companies if you play ball. And by the way, I still have the photos of you with your mistress."

After a pause, "Great, I knew I could count on you."

*   *   *

It was time for Michael to start recruiting experts to volunteer for the mission. The project was on a strictly need-to-know basis, so this was delicate. The more people knew, the more likely the secrets would get out.

"Gentlemen and ladies, you were briefed. We are preparing a manned mission to another planet that supports life. Let me state my bias up front: I think our chances for success are much improved if the explorers we send on this mission are the planners and engineers themselves, so they have already thought of potential problems that could arise and how to deal with them. This project is secret and that's as much as I can tell you unless and until any of you volunteer, so if you aren't sure, or you don't want to risk extended space flight, please leave now. You may have heard rumors. Assume they have some foundation. That's as much as I can tell you. I hope all of you will consider volunteering for this mission and for astronaut training. Wallace, let me ask you first. What's your opinion?"

This was music to the ears of Charles Wallace, a microbiologist. He always fantasized about being an astronaut, going into space. Sometimes he even dared to imagine he was a national space hero like Flash Packard. But he knew this new reality might not live up to the fantasy.

"If the destination planet has biosignatures, it's flora and fauna will probably be very different from life here. We will learn so much. Even if the biology is similar, that would also tell us a great deal. Seriously, there is a real potential we will encounter poisonous biological substances, incompatible biochemistry, bacteria or protozoa that colonize our gut and produce toxins, bacteria that potentially infect and kill us and the plants we introduce. We need to take along and breed test animals, rats and mice, to try the air, the food, everything first."

Michael was alarmed. "Just a minute, we have a chance to start with a clean slate and you propose sending vermin to the new planet?"

"No, no, you misunderstand me. I'm not suggesting we send politicians, although using them as test animals *would* give them a useful purpose in life."

"What, then?"

"I'm not interested in surviving a dangerous space odyssey just to get poisoned by some weird microbe or eaten by some monster or being a host for some strange parasite when I arrive.

"If there is anything dangerous there we can't avoid or isolate, I would feel better take neutron beam weapons to wipe it out without harming the surroundings. Then we can sort out the ecological consequences, and figure out whether destroying the threat disrupted any natural cycles. You know, if we can do any bioforming on the planet before we get there it would greatly improve our odds of success."

"I'm afraid there isn't time for that. We need an inventory of the possible dangers that could be lurking and have a plan for each one. Part of your job. Don't we have some experience with this already from our artificial life experiments?"

"That's right. We've learned a lot but I don't know if it will help us now."

"Newman, what do you think? Are you interested?"

Van Newman, an AI/robotics specialist replied, "We'll need mini-robots to do critical and dangerous work. But you already know about the training issues and limitations. There is a very real danger that robots could inadvertently destroy the mission or accidentally kill the astronauts. I can think of measures we might take to minimize that risk, checks and balances on the machines, sanity checks and the like. If you wish, I will prepare a presentation for you laying out what I think we can do and why."

"Thank you, I will be waiting for your report. Evelyn, do you have anything to add?"

Evelyn G. Wallace, climatologist, wife of Charles Wallace, answered, "Do we know anything about the weather, how the land is arranged, the ocean and atmospheric circulation patterns, climate zones? Is there any way to assess regional climates, where can we live on the new planet that suits us, where the productive growing areas are, where to avoid flood-prone, cyclone-prone, drought-prone, and other problem spots? Do we know the places where the weather is most hospitable and gives us the best chance of establishing the first colony?"

"All good questions, but we only have limited data and computer simulations at this point. Dr. Osler, what are your concerns? I would like to mention to everyone that Dr. Osler will be doing the general health and cardiovascular screening for anyone who volunteers for this mission."

Elizabeth Osler, MD, was Titian's expert in space medicine. "As everyone is aware, the cumulative effect of high-energy radiation and charged particles over many decades is a serious concern. Even some of the astronauts we've sent to the moons of the giant planets received enough radiation to develop cancers. Radiation and particle shielding is paramount. I am also working on a report. We at least have practical data from this experience. We know we need advance drones to sample the air and water to see if it is toxic. Are the micronutrients, vitamins, digestible minerals, amino acids, and fats we need present on the surface? What produces them? A few simple light weight micro probes that float to the surface might tell us. Is there a plan B if the primary target planet is a no-go? This is essential knowledge and I will be working with our biologists on this."

From their interstellar micro-probes, they already knew their spacecraft had to be long and skinny, they needed particle shields that would gradually erode away, and they had to manage the enormous heat generated on the leading edge of spacecraft. They could use water tanks or other shielding methods along the sides, despite the weight penalty which they had to minimize. There were also superconducting split toroidal magnetic shields and other techniques to consider.

"Okay. Dr. Jenner, can you add anything?"

Dr. Renee Jenner, was an immunologist and researcher. She said that "If there are any kinds of harmful bugs, toxins, or substances, we have to develop ways to immunize the crew against them, to neutralize them. If there is a way to get samples from the new planet's surface and analyze them before we land, that would be great."

Was there a way for the advance probes to do chemical and biological testing? Weight is always critical, but could they develop a fully equipped, lightweight minilab to produce anti-toxins, anti-virals, and anti-bacterials? Could a robot isolate and neutralize every deadly microorganism and virus it could find? Dr. Jenner considered this to be a life-or-death matter, and everyone agreed.

And then there was the matter of feeding themselves. "Norman, how do we know what to eat, and how do we get a balanced diet," Thor asked.

Norman Carson, a well-known agriculturist, replied, "It begins with soil testing. We should concentrate on bringing hybrid seeds, as many varieties as possible, and as tolerant as possible. It will be a matter of experiment to see what survives. Then we can harvest the seeds from whatever grows, but first we have to make sure our plants don't absorb harmful chemicals or organisms from the soil."

Cross-breeding with native plants was out of the question at first, until they knew what they were doing. Real farming wouldn't be possible until the second or third year. They might have to try to find ways to manufacture food and nutrients from native plants. They should take all of the freeze-dried bacteria they need for soil culture, just in case. They should also take plants and microbes to introduce to displace native species. It could turn out that they want to bring about the extinction of competing native microbes, since the genetic mechanisms are not likely to be compatible. That would be a do-it-yourself, on-the-fly bioforming.

They concluding the meeting by setting up follow-on individual meetings.

Afterwards, Evelyn talked to her husband in the hallway.

She told her husband, "You always fantasized about being an astronaut. This is your big chance."

Charles hesitated, "But it's a one-way mission. Will you come with me? What if we decide to have children?"

"How responsible is it to stay here and have children destined to freeze and die in outer space before they even grow up? Yes, we'll go together to the new planet."

John Forbes was talking to his girlfriend Renee Jenner, also in the hallway. "What do you make of that?"

"Starting our own new planet? It's not an everyday opportunity," she replied.

Forbes complained as usual, "We die in space either here or there. Do you know what the chances of survival are on this new planet? There will be natives who will spear us and cook us in some oven. That's if we're still alive after we're cryogenically revived. In that case I'm sure they're used to frozen food, too."

Jenner tried to convince him. "So, we can all be pigs in space, then in the oven. It's still better than our chances of surviving here."

"Don't you know I'm prone to freezer burn?"

"Then you'll just have to be very particular about how you are frozen."

"I want to have some fun before I freeze to death. I'm not so sure I want to end my life with years of training and hard work."

"Come on, you have to have the right spirit. Look forward to the adventure and some new experiences. Enjoy the challenge of solving tough problems. Think about how much we can learn. Then you will have fun getting prepared." It was clear Jenner wanted to go, and she wanted her boyfriend to be as enthusiastic as she was.

*　　*　　*

Thor addressed the current and potential astronauts along with the project staff. Those briefings that were absolutely essential were normally conducted weekly in one of Titian's conference rooms on a need-to-know basis. The rooms were dingy interior spaces equipped with state-of-the-art projectors and visual aids.

"Ladies and gentlemen, you all know me by now. This is the first of our weekly briefings I will provide on the mission status, problems, and milestones. Please stay awake and think about what I am saying.

"Time is short. We have a lot to do to be successful. Everything has to be absolutely right including the crew. Don't ignore the details, because if we omit even one small but essential item, it could potentially condemn the mission to disaster. I not only expect, but insist, that each and every one of you be involved in the design and development, and to have at least working knowledge of every subsystem.

"This project is Titian's highest priority. It's also secret. Not even the board of directors know what we are doing, they only know a cover story. They think it's just another ambitious space mission. So let's keep everything among ourselves to avoid outside interference. Always identify problems early, because we don't have time to back track." The meeting concluded after reviewing the requirements, feasibility studies, strategies, subsystems, schedules, next steps, test plans, and so forth.

The project was divided up into as many parallel efforts as possible, including life support, propulsion, magnetic sail, cryogenics, habitat, magnetic radiation shield, remote deceleration and landing, artificial intelligence applications and robotics, biologic packages, probes, and essential machinery, plus vital subsystems such as power, heat management, communications, and so on. There was debate about carrying standard laser/neutron beam weapons in case those proved necessary.

Research continued studying microgravity, radiation shielding, frozen embryo preservation, suspended animation, and cryogenic techniques, most of it supported by other government contracts.

Thor was not at liberty to talk about propulsion and space elevators, since most of that development was being conducted under secret government military contracts. Nor could he talk about ongoing experimental development of Majorana particle matter-antimatter thruster systems, which might not be ready in time anyway. Same with some materials and other related research and development. Stephen Lee, a physicist also involved with this project, was involved in some of this other research.

The final plan was to send explorers to the two closest potentially habitable planets. Three expeditions would travel to the closest planet, taking different routes and arriving at 4-month intervals. As a contingency, they could divert to the next closest promising triple star system and hope they were lucky enough to find a suitable planet there. Three more expeditions would fly to the farther planet on different routes, also arriving at 4-month intervals. In this case, the contingency plan was to divert to the alternate yellow dwarf if necessary and hope to find a suitable planet there. Four small micro-probe fleets, designed to detect various problems, launched toward target and alternate planets, arriving year ahead of the habitats, could give an automated signal to divert while astronauts and embryos were still in a state of suspended animation. Prior to the launches, data collection on these and other possible systems would continue.

And nobody, including Thor, knew how much time they had before society broke down.

*   *   *

Annie was busy elsewhere.

She was speaking to a coworker at a sleazy bar near the office. "Hey, Carl, I see from my social media page it's your birthday today. Why don't we celebrate after work? I'll buy you a drink, then maybe we can think of a suitable birthday present..."

At another bar a few days later, Annie asked an executive from a competing company, "You buying the drinks tonight, Ralph?"

"Yeah, I guess so."

"How can I possibly repay you? Maybe we can come up with something at your place..."

The next week in an upscale hotel room, Annie asked a prospective customer's attorney, "Well, Johnny, you say you once made a fortune suing insurance companies?"

"Yeah, they couldn't stop me. I'm was like a bulldog. I never gave up. That was the springboard to my current position."

"I'll bet you're used to getting your way..."

Work on the fleet of spacecraft continued at a feverish pace during the next several years. There would only be one shot at success, and a lot of new ground had to be broken. Rumors were afloat, same as always, about a death star, an errant black hole, a Nibiru. The true data and the facts remained classified top secret, and the rumors were dismissed by most. People went about their business.

Meanwhile, Titian maintained half a dozen giant chemical rockets with their nuclear payloads, ready for immediate use against Invader when the time was right politically, that is, when the rumors became mainstream. Titian was well paid for this effort, and Annie received sizable commissions, so all was right with the world.

*   *   *

Because of time lags, the condition of the target planets could not be known in advance. A hypernova or nearby nova or supernova, a massive stellar flare, a wandering black hole, a gamma ray burst aimed at the planet, or some other cataclysm could irradiate any habitat before the explorers got there. The target planet could experience super volcanic eruptions or some other environmental disaster. The size and frequency of Oort cloud disturbances, and the presence of asteroid belts for these planets were unknowns, so a massive meteor or comet impact was always possible. There could be continental drift and climate episodes such as a snow-ball or sauna planet. Not to mention environmental and biological poisons and hazards. These, and other potentially serious problems, however likely or unlikely, meant that the astronauts couldn't be sure of what they would find when they got to their destination.

Historically, colonies on newly discovered continents and islands often failed because there just weren't enough colonists to make a go of it. So, were they sending a critical mass of astronaut settlers, embryos, and robots, plus extras in case of diseases and disasters?

There was also the loose cannon named Conway traveling on one of the six ships. If he survived the trip, since he expected absolute, dictatorial power, the best course of action was for everyone to ignore him and program the robots to do the same.

*   *   *

Dedication can sometimes spring from conceit, especially if it is cultural conceit. While they weren't building pyramids, this was best expressed by Thor at one of the weekly status meetings.

"You are all well aware we have to get this right. It's our only hope for perpetual survival. If our species dies out, something unique and precious will be lost forever. Our species has survived and prospered everywhere on this planet. We painfully evolved a culture to a state of near perfection over many millennia, extended our knowledge and mastery over all the realms of nature and purified our genes through the Canaille and super-volcanic periods. It is inconceivable that there will ever be any other creature or culture like us anywhere else in the universe. We have a moral obligation and a destiny to spread ourselves all over the galaxy. I'm proud to have a role in this mission and know that all of you feel the same."

Skinner decided to have some fun and be the wet blanket. "Honestly, Thor. I'm not so sure we will be perpetuating anything. Another planet with different niches, different flora and fauna, differing physical environment, will bring out and evolve different behaviors in us, and we will also evolve new physical forms to adapt. We will change and evolve and not remain the same. Our culture will change, too. What we are here and now will become a fading memory. Why don't we forget all this stress, take it easy, and just launch a few hundred museums as our memorial to all the corners of the galaxy?"

Thor ignored Skinner's smart remarks and persisted anyway. "It's not just about skills and culture. For the greatest adaptability, you have to have the right mix of instincts and character traits plus a sufficiently diverse gene pool. We already have that."

Skinner elaborated. "True. All jokes and tail-twisting aside, we will change. We are talking about evolving archetypes that will force the change. An archetype is more than an instinctive behavior pattern enforced by emotional attraction or repulsion around which memory and other cognitive processes are organized. It is a deeply subconscious general, non-specific, pattern that takes form and expression through cultural and individual experience. For example, there are social archetypes such as social reciprocity that everyone shares (you scratch my back, I'll scratch yours), archetypes for mental functioning such as cognitive dissonance and an intolerance of inconsistency in others, language and mental play such as affinity for rhyming and wordplay, and for jokes based on incongruities and logical inconsistencies, and so on. These archetypes guide mental, verbal, social, and other play that help people to learn and develop survival skills.

"There are also the 'traditional' archetypes or instincts if you will. Examples showing why we need a range of them are mother-child and father-child relationships. The mother can be a witch, so that the child is forced to live for the benefit of its mother and emotionally nourish her, do whatever she wants. The energy goes from child to mother so the child is drained. Conversely, the fairy godmother spoils the child and gives it everything it desires, but in the process she becomes drained. All of the energy goes from mother to child. The child behaves according to the corresponding archetype of either 'orphan' or 'golden child' (which in the extreme case is the totally spoiled child). Similar paternal archetypes are the despotic dictator (as in 'my way or the highway') where the child must do and be what the father demands and jump at his every command. The energy goes from the child to the father. On the other hand, the mentor or teacher can concern himself with the child or student's development, providing it with the full benefit of his knowledge and experience so the energy goes from father to child; for the positive father archetype nothing is more satisfying than passing on his accumulated knowledge and experience.

Page 47

"Clearly, you always need a wise mixture in each case. Like Annie, anyone raised by a nanny-bot will have mental deficiencies. Their instincts won't complement robotic behavior, so they won't develop properly. That's why the mission should never consist only of embryos raised by nanny-bots. We have to include astronauts.

"People commonly wonder why other people and cultures are capable of incongruent extremes. The same hand that rocks a baby to sleep can also wage war and slaughter an enemy or a rival. Someone who is flattering to his boss will turn around and badmouth coworkers to their face or behind their backs. There are serial rapists and murderers who are nice to their families and friends so nobody ever suspected them. I could on. For the sake of adaptability and survival, archetypes enable and bring about these polar opposites of behavior. Extreme behavior can adapt people to extreme conditions, but that also means everyone is doomed to both internal and external conflicts, guilt, and angst. Interestingly enough, there are other archetypes that drive manipulators and con-men to instinctively take advantage of that same guilt and angst.

"Not only that, there is always a danger of pathological archetypal possession. That means that an archetype, or actually a belief, habit, or an obsession rooted in an archetype, takes over the entire mental apparatus. A person becomes fixated on one thing. This is an unconscious process and its outside manifestation is an obsession, a one-track mind that will just not let go until something else at least as powerful and archetypal as the obsession forcefully displaces it. We all know this is dangerous and destructive, and it prevents the clear-headed thinking needed to address novel situations. It's also a component of mob behavior. If our mission leaders become obsessed this way, including becoming drunk with power, or possessed by the alpha male instinct, our mission will fail."

"Do you have anyone in particular in mind?" someone asked.

Skinner concluded, "You know who I'm talking about. I could elaborate on this for the next month, but you get the general idea so I will spare you."

The warning applied to both people and intelligent robots.

Skinner's implication was that contradictions are built in to everyone's mind and this facilitates adaptability, if not mental health. The potential for obsessing on one extreme of the contradiction is always there. Sooner or later, under the right conditions, that's a formula for disaster. They had to guard against one-track obsessions.

"Let me add one other note that could trip us up," Skinner added. "All human values ultimately spring from archetypes as made real, interpreted, and expressed through culture and individual experience. Therefore, the culture we take with us to another planet is crucial but it has to be flexible and we have to be open to adaptation. It is difficult to identify absolute natural values. I'm not saying there aren't any, in fact, I think that there are.

"All of this is to say that being physically prepared is not enough. We have to prepare mentally or we will fail, and that's even tougher. Please think about it. At some point we have to add it to our preparation."

Thor ended the discussion. It was the close of the workweek, they were all exhausted from the long days, and it was time to take a break.

There was a real concern that Annie would sabotage the entire effort. Thor wondered, should they give Annie credit for the whole project so she would lose credibility if she tried to stop it? After all, she tries to take credit for everything she sells to the customers and everything she gets involved with anyway.

But Michael's response to the idea was, "That won't work. In the end, the old man takes credit for everything that's successful in this outfit, not to mention blaming you for whatever goes wrong. Let's find a way to get Annie a big fat obscene commission from the project. Any ideas?"

Annie could not be allowed to sell seats on the spacecraft, or get paid under-the-table for funneling inside information. In fact there had to be some penalty for any kind of sabotage. She wouldn't hesitate to poison the well if there was something in it for her. Maybe commissions could be arranged for subcontracts under some pretext, which wouldn't even have to be credible. This, plus a penalty for divulging confidential information like the loss of commissions or the loss of her security clearance. There could be no loopholes for her to take advantage of.

*   *   *

Progress continued on the habitat, enhanced magnetic sail, incremental fusion reactor system, galactic particle shielding, heat dispersal system, magnetic radiation shield, a proposed virus detection and dispersal apparatus, propulsion, mitigation of microgravity effects, minimum physical stimulation for astronauts to prevent atrophy, ergonomics, the landing system, the psychology of working in cramped spaces, and a myriad of other details.

Stephen Lee speculated with Osler, Thor, and Carson concerning the deployment of miles-long micro-thin composite ribbons to radiate away reactor heat, as was also being used on some other spacecraft. Perhaps they could find a radiating material for the ribbons, maybe a ceramic-semiconductor-rare earth-silver or copper laminate, that could also act as a thermocouple to generate electricity? Thermocouples make very inefficient electric generators, but with miles of ribbons maybe they could generate enough extra power in deep space to maintain a strong magnetic field to deflect charged particles. After all, there was an enormous temperature gradient between the super-heated leading edge of a fast-moving spacecraft and the cold of interstellar space. If it worked, it could help prevent astronauts from getting their butts French fried by cosmic rays during the journey.

Unfortunately, Lee was not going to be an astronaut, as much as he wanted to. He had two aging parents in poor health to take care of. He also hoped he would have a chance to reconcile with an estranged son before it was too late.

These were still the "normal" times. Rumors grew and flew, but both the government and Titian had every incentive to keep the truth hidden, confused, and censored as long as possible. For now, business and research could still proceed normally, and progress at

Titian was swift. How long might this last before everything went crazy? Nobody knew.

*　　*　　*

Eight years later, some viewers were tuned in to a nightly talk show with host Roy and his sidekick Mack.

Roy asked, "So Annie, you worked for Titian. What can you tell us about Invader? Is it real? Is it just a persistent rumor? What will happen?"

"I can tell you it's irrevocable. This planet will fly into outer space and freeze in another four years. That's why I quit. Why should any of us slave away in some awful job when the future is limited? I deserve better, don't you? Now is the time to have what you've always wanted. Time for YOLO. We don't need to be spending money on space programs, armies, bureaucracies and red tape, pollution controls, schools and universities, science, research. None of that matters anymore. There is no future in any of it. Give the money to the people. I know I deserve to have a big mansion, a luxury car, fashionable clothes, and satchels full of money to spend. Don't you? Drink, get fat, be happy. There are people with more stuff than they can ever use. Take it for the less fortunate people. Give it to the ones that need it. Let them live it up for once. Anyone with a brain can see that."

Roy, intervening, "Some of us like what we do and don't intend to quit."

"Are you crazy or something? I happen to know you like your booze and fast cars. You have a whole garage full of them. You're nuts to just sit here and run your mouth every single night. Why are you laughing, Mac? You think this is a joke? This is no joke. Wake up. It's time for you to get out and do everything you ever wanted to do. There are no consequences anymore. What can they do to you, sentence you to die? You'll die anyway. What about your car collection? How long has it been since you drove them all?"

Mac, still laughing: "There *are* times when I'm not drinking and think, what about my family? Don't you think we still have to be responsible?"

Annie was getting irritated as usual. "Just when do you ever put your bottle down? You're insane if you can't see this. Aren't you listening? It just doesn't matter anymore! Why can't you understand that? Your whole family should just go and have a good time."

Roy stepped in. "And now, time for our next guest after this message."

The cat was out of the bag. Sooner rather than later, everyone will be forced to decide whether to cope. Some will look for a refuge. Others will look for an escape. Still others will seek to make peace with God. Like Annie, many will choose to live it up right to the end and then let fate take its course. Plenty of people will just try to avoid a decision and stoically wait, or remain in denial as long as they can.

*   *   *

A week later as Thor was driving home, he could hear the sermon on the radio in the background.

"The time to choose is here and now. The path diverges directly in front of us. Which road will you travel? Trying times lie ahead. Every relationship, every quality, every fiber will be tested. Will you be responsible or irresponsible? Selfish or selfless? Will you prove worthy of life or worthy of death? Redemption or damnation? Eternity is upon us. How will you choose to spend yours? Pray for strength, we must be as one..."

Millions were tuned in. Rev. Franklin was inspiring his minions, repeating and refining his message until it became second nature to him and his followers.

Maybe some good advice there, Thor thought.

Thor was certain support for the Titian's space program would now wane as people focused more and more on their own fate. Annie would add to that. If he could somehow glamorize the program, make it a ray of hope to a condemned world, counterbalance Annie's relentless calls to pull the funding, live it up, and distribute some to the people, maybe public funding and Titian's reserve funding could continue long enough to ensure the project's completion.

It occurred to Thor that an endorsement from Rev. Franklin would go a long way towards prolonging support for the mission. He contacted Rock Peters, The Reverend's right-hand man.

Thor told Peters, "The Reverend's lessons don't have to end with the death of this planet. His message can travel with us to the habitable reaches of the galaxy. Conway and Titian have plans to expand from this planet to at least two others. And it could continue from there. How can you not want your message to enlighten many future generations well beyond our small world? It's a noble mission. All we ask is your public expressions of support."

Peters answered, "I will think about it and make a recommendation to Reverend Franklin."

Thor concluded, "Thank you. That's all I ask."

Chapter Five
At the Museum

All societies have their important "myths", that is, stories originating from their history, stories that define their self-image and who they are, stories explaining their origins and destiny, stories illustrating expected moral standards and what the society should value and devalue. They are stories that give meaning to life in the society.

Think of the American wild west, along with resourceful, brave, self-sufficient frontiersmen, tales of cowboys and Indians, and a history of fierce individualism. Or think of the evolution of Nazism in Germany and subsequent collective guilt; or of the pride and purpose and sense of divine destiny inspired by grand projects like the building the pyramids.

Naturally, societal "myths" influence various members and classes of society differently, sometimes very differently. These beliefs and values can be discerned in Thor's beliefs and statements to the key project members, and in the sense of purpose, dedication, determination, and actions of the group.

And these beliefs and values impacted what happened next.

*   *   *

Leah, age 7, was anxious. "Mommy, are we really going on a train?"

Jenna Hurlock answered, "Yes, Leah. In another hour we will be leaving on the express train. It's really fast. You'll love it! Cities, farms, factories, mountains, rivers and so many other things will fly past the windows."

"Oh Mommy! I why can't we go right now? I've never been on a train. Teddy got to go on a train once, but I didn't get to go."

"That's because you're a girl. They don't like girls on their trains," Ted, age 11, piped in. "Girls have cooties."

"Be nice and stop teasing your sister. You know better," Jenna admonished Ted.

"Yeah. You better be nice to me," Leah shot back.

"One day I'll have a toy train, just like the big train." Ted continued. "I'll play with it every day. It will have buildings and people and bridges and everything."

Leah asked. "Can I ride on your train?"

Ted teased her again, "You can be the train maid and clean the cars."

Jenna had enough. "Ted, I told you not to tease your sister. Toy trains are expensive, and we can't afford one. Both of you behave so we can all have a good time," Jenna said. "We don't get to travel much. In a few hours we'll be at the museum. There's a lot for both of you to see and learn, and I want you to pay attention."

The museum was a kind of shrine, with displays and artifacts explaining the history of the Canaille. And every Canaille felt a duty, an obligation, to make a pilgrimage there at some point before reaching adulthood. Then they could understand better who they were and where they were going. It evolved into a tradition and had become a point of pride.

The large, modern, brownstone museum was located in a big city that anyone could visit. It had not been built in a Canaille settlement because regular people would never want to go there.

The Hurlocks were a typical Canaille family. They lived in a typical Canaille rectangular tract house with three bedrooms, one and a half baths, a living room, a small kitchen, a dining area they barely fit into, and a full but unfinished basement. Chipper Hurlock had an old, barely functional, standard-sized junker for a car, but they didn't use it that often. Convenient public transportation was readily available. They were taking a bus to the train station to start their trip.

Chipper was a former civil engineer, now a teacher like his wife, and he carried that over into his private life, providing advice and encouragement to those around him. Unconsciously, he wanted others to acknowledge and appreciate this quality, and to like him for it. He made it a point to follow through on whatever he promised and hated to disappoint or alienate anyone. He liked to be with others, and hated being alone. Problems and poor treatment that would irritate others just rolled off his back and slipped from his mind. He tended to be a peacemaker. He wanted everything to go smoothly and would do what he could to make that happen. He was easy-going, took things as they came, and avoided looking too far beneath the surface.

Jenna was spontaneous, warm, outgoing, and attentive. She was practical and had her share of common sense. She was not a deep thinker and didn't ask a lot of questions, but just took the present for what it was, preferably in the company of family and friends.

A few hours later they arrived at the museum. As soon as they moved up a few spots in the ticket line another patron shouted at them, "Hey you four, get in the back of the line. Who do you think you are? Canaille trash." This was typical treatment, but they still resented it.

Canaille history was redefined with the creation of the Universal Security Administration. Brandon Cathcart was its director; Joseph Huber was the Deputy Director.

Just beyond the entrance there were exhibits that used AI bots to recreate Security Administration speeches given to unions and other organizations, along with some correspondence and conversations based on official records.

The featured exhibit was an AI reproduction of Cathcart giving his celebrated historic speech to an assembled crowd near an outdoor monument:

"Our civilization has enemies everywhere on this planet. These enemies must be found. They must be pursued. They must be defeated. Even now, new terrorists are emerging, new bombs are being built, and a reign of destruction is being planned against us. Subversives and domestic enemies abound that will destroy us without mercy if we allow it. They are troublemakers dedicated to subversive creeds and forms of government like fascism or social democracy or Catholicism or meritocracy. They are a diverse gang of subversives, misguided activists, pacifists, gypsies, Mormons, Amish, and fundamentalists who refuse to conform to the programs, norms, and philosophy of the State, and who resolutely reject necessary State control. These miscreants are rife with agitators who foment destructive riots and disturb the peace for their own nefarious ends. There are journalists outside the approved big media companies who spread lies and dangerous doctrines contradicting the State and encourage this unrest and discord. We must protect ourselves from these subversives or they will soon destroy our way of life."

Cathcart continued, "In spite of what our enemies claim, the computer systems and artificial intelligence at our disposal is nothing more than a human relations database. It should be viewed as just another form of social media, harmless in itself. This agency respects the truth and would never misuse any incidental information that happens our way during our critical mission to protect you, the people.

"The State is the collective wisdom, the highest form of organization, and there must be nothing above or outside the State. It embodies the collective wisdom that acts on behalf of the people. The genius of the State is the eternal form that must rule over everything. The will of the leader of the State is the law of the land. All companies, professions, unions, bureaucracies, and markets must work together to ensure the success of the State as guided by the enlightened foresight of its duly appointed leader. Resistance to this natural order by any organization, individual, or jurisdiction cannot be tolerated as a matter of principle. The State *is* you, the people, and as such claims to the right to force the principles of just government on all people and institutions of this great planet. Consequently, the entire world is moving inexorably toward a blessed state of unification without exception. Therefore, it is an absurdity to speak of 'provincial sovereignty' or 'individual sovereignty' or 'group sovereignty.' The State transforms every organization and individual as an instrument of the greatest good. The State is the light shining in the darkness, it is the way forward, it speaks for all the people, and it shall not be overcome."

The next historical re-creation depicted Huber and Cathcart talking in a 3D projection of Cathcart's office, a grandiose affair more like a palace library.

Huber stated, privately, "As you know, we have an archive on every politician from prime ministers down to the councilmen in the smallest towns, not just on this continent but on every continent and island throughout the world. Indeed, we have built a nearly completed computerized dossier on the entire world's population. Habits, inclinations, friendships and relationships, sexual preferences and aberrations, promiscuities, affairs, underworld contacts, drug use legal or otherwise, alcoholic and other addictions, crimes factual or alleged, reported and unreported irregularities including skimming, bribery and misuse of funds, gossip and scandal and all manner of scurrilous information, psychiatric visits, secrets of every sort, research and reading habits, it's all in there and more. We have the full social network and details and contents of every communication for every single individual. We watch the private lives of everyone on the planet like so many germs in a microscope. We have the means to fabricate tales about our enemies, rivals, and anyone we don't like, and make it believable.

"There is no public or private computer, phone, social medium, TV, appliance, satellite, microwave link, fiber cable, car, train, bus, library, surveillance system, robot, point-of-sale device, camera, RFID tag, diary, or electronic device of any kind anywhere in the world we haven't tapped into. And it's all processed by supercomputers and Artificial Intelligence systems that automatically produce dossiers on everyone without exception.

"We can easily disrupt and sabotage any activity that doesn't suit us and point the finger at whomever we want to.

"We are truly omniscient and on the largest scale. We have absolute power and control. We are the envy of the gods.

"You will recall, Cathcart, there was once time when the Investigation Bureau and the Intelligence Agency spied on a famous Canaille leader. We tried to blackmail him with information we collected and then altered. We bugged his home and hotel rooms, spied on his associates, and smeared him as a communist and a philanderer in an attempt to either end his career or drive him to suicide. He was a strong personality and resisted our coercion. It's embarrassing how crude our methods were at the time. We've come a long way since then. We can break anybody these days. We will always prevail."

Cathcart responded, "But you know we can never relax. We can't afford the merest gossip or complaint against us; it can always escalate into a full-blown movement. Subversive talk and thoughts must be immediately crushed. All the while keeping our activity hidden behind the scenes."

"That's never been a problem," Huber said. "When we disappear someone, infect them with a secret virus, overdose them, use a brain scrambler on them to make them senile, nobody can prove it's anything but natural causes."

"But some people will look for the worst and then rumors can start," Cathcart observed. "We will know of course, and we have to nip it in the bud. Besides, our AI74B master AI computer analyzes everything and maintains lists of potential trouble makers, even if they aren't causing any trouble or doing anything overly suspicious right at the moment."

"I'm afraid the list keeps getting longer," Huber noted. "The has grown to fifteen per cent of the population by now. Critical mass is ten per cent."

Cathcart concurred, "Yes, I have made my own inquiries and come up with similar numbers. I have an idea and I've been talking to our Biological Control Section. What we want is to make the trouble makers, if not the entire population, docile. Anyone who resists will be disposed of. I will fill you in on the details as soon as BCS gets back to me."

The next simulation recorded the official plan.

"Here is our objective and our plan," Cathcart stated. "First, we will identify every actual and potential troublemaker planetwide. The most powerful political leaders at the provincial and national levels will be prioritized. We can easily control local leaders with our usual methods. They will all do as we command without hesitation, then the rest of the population will follow like sheep, since most of them always look for a shepherd to follow and have no capability for leadership themselves. We, as the State, are of course the shepherd. We want to eliminate the power-seeking alpha male archetype from this segment of the population, and enhance any archetypes that foster dependencies. We also want to suppress any instincts for curiosity or questioning or even critical examination of authority. I have instructed BCS to proceed at maximum speed to develop a virus that will alter the target population's genetic makeup and gene expression accordingly. They assure me they can design and produce that virus in sufficient quantity. We can use the same mechanisms to distribute the viruses we've used in the past to give diseases to troublemakers that have to be silenced. There will be collateral damage, of course, but we don't care about that. The gene-altered people will become useful as a blue-collar work force, agency police and bodyguards, and spies for the State."

*   *   *

Chipper enlightened his children, "We Canaille were a target and we are the products of that genetic experiment gone wrong. You see, genetics, epigenetics, and behavior are much more complex and subtle than Cathcart's simple-minded view. He saw everything as simply a threat to be directly controlled or squashed. Those were the glasses he was wearing."

There had to be unintended consequences. Changing or suppressing one behavior results in compensatory changes in the intensity of other complementary behaviors and biological systems. It's like a rubber sheet. If you pull it in one direction it compensates by shrinking in the other. Diminishing Canaille leadership ability along with increasing their dependency and attraction to a leader sharpened their sense of fairness and equal treatment which they expect from those leaders, and it greatly heightened the potential for rage, resentment, and anger when fair treatment was not forthcoming. That turned out to have far-reaching consequences. Instead of turning the Canaille into a bunch of sheep, they became much more like wolves in sheep's clothing.

It wasn't long before the Canaille figured out what had been perpetrated on them. The victims of the virus naturally started to feel really strange. For one thing, they felt lost, no longer having a sense of purpose. Work groups floundered, needing direction from bosses at the top. Many of the Canaille became short-tempered. Many lost their sense of well-being. In the back of their minds, some wanted a savior to release them from the unfamiliar and unpleasant feelings. Religion made a comeback, and most people made a new commitment to spiritual life and old-fashioned values. That's one reason Reverend Franklin has such a large following among the Canaille. It was clear at the time something just wasn't right. They became more attracted than normal to demagogues, rosy promises, miracle cures. And as the reality of what had happened became widespread, a hurricane of resentment and anger was unleashed.

*　*　*

The Hurlocks continued to the next exhibit.

It was a picture of Dr. Schoen, a virologist, and a 3D holograph of his rather ordinary-looking laboratory. Dr. Schoen was a Canaille and the first to investigate the virus. He wanted to find out what was wrong with himself and his friends and family.

The exhibit simulated the doctor in his lab talking to his assistant.

"Dr. Schoen, it's difficult to grow this virus. It doesn't replicate very well. Instead of causing the cell to reproduce the virus until the cell bursts like every other virus I've seen, it seems to be self-limiting and to only make a few thousand copies that penetrate the cell membrane and spread through the blood."

"I see that all of the samples with this virus create similar DNA changes to the same half-dozen genes."

"What genes are those?"

"They control behavior."

"I've never heard of a virus that acts that way."

"It's not a natural virus in any way. I believe this has to be a weaponized virus that acts like that. I've heard that government labs can make viruses that kill or cripple slowly without many symptoms at first, so they spread more widely before they burn themselves out, and they have other viruses that multiply and kill very quickly but don't disperse widely. I think we're dealing with something similar here. It has the fingerprints of something intentional and unnatural."

Rumors about the new virus spread like wildfire. Anger and rage blossomed exponentially among everyone who suspected they had been infected, amplified by their new genetic makeup. They became like a scattering of iron filings waiting for a magnet. And when a magnet arrived, it would sweep people up into a focused machine perusing an unknown end, and impel them to powerful action in behalf of a cause they at first had no real conscious awareness of. The situation was primed and ready with unconscious anticipation. It felt like something was about to happen. It was the precursor to a vast uncontrollable mob.

The first display in the next exhibit room was an old enlarged, sprawling aerial photograph. It showed a hilly terrain with a small complex of similar, plain high-rise office buildings near the top of one hill and a smaller fenced and gated military base with an airport and two crossed runways at the top of another nearby hill. A tall gated and guarded fence surrounded the office complex.

It was a military base near the Universal Security Administration's headquarters and computer center. The base was also within defendable distance of the Administration's backup center in the hilly terrain 200 miles away. The overall military Chief of Staff, Lieutenant General Hines, had his headquarters on the base. Air wing commander Brigadier General Clarke reported directly to Hines. Cathcart thought he had total control over both generals, and their first priority was his defense. Both generals were under Cathcart's thumb. He was blackmailing them. In theory, the military reported to the Prime Minister, but Cathcart was the power behind the throne who really ran everything. The military base was an important element of protection for the Administration, so it had to be under the Administration's control.

There was an AI reconstruction of a meeting Gen. Hines had with his staff: "As you know from my voicemail, we are going to have another training exercise next week, so I want all of you to prepare and submit your preliminary plan in two days. The scenario this time is that four invading automated aircraft will attempt to penetrate the Universal Security Administration headquarters and backup facility and launch their missiles into these complexes. We will be using real aircraft with dummy weapons. This will be followed by a ground invasion by combat robots attempting to breach the 'softened' perimeter. Dummy foot soldiers will follow the robots. You must intercept the invading aircraft, and anticipate and counter the possible ground action to follow. I will not give you any additional details because you must be prepared for any contingency in your plan. Any questions? Dismissed."

In the next re-creation, Gen. Clarke was speaking quietly in a crawlspace somewhere on the base. "Did all of you sneak in out of the view of the cameras, were you ultra-careful?" Eight others all nodded.

"Good. This spot is farthest from any microphones inside this building. The opportunity we have been waiting for is finally here. You are the best geeks in the business. The success of this operation is in your hands. As far as I can determine, Security Admin has not detected us. Hines is acting a little funny to me, or maybe it's my imagination, but he hasn't said anything. Have you 3D printed all of the computer chips we need and done all of the simulation tests we talked about?"

Everyone nodded.

"Good. The aircraft and weapons will be in for maintenance tomorrow prior to the exercise. Substitute the new chips for the originals. Destroy the originals so they can't be traced. We need chips for four F92 fighter bombers, eight air-to-ground missiles on each F92, and one round-penetrating nuclear bunker buster bomb on each. The bunker busters are not part of the exercise, but the other generals will just figure they are a curve Hines is throwing them to deal with. All the weapons must appear to be dummies from their transponders like we discussed. The hidden firmware script will be as follows: Two of the F92s will fly treetop level to the backup center at just subsonic, twenty minutes away. After they are in the air at least fifteen minutes, the other two 92s will fly to Admin HQ. The bunker buster tactical nukes drop first, one on the computer complex and one on the main office building at each complex. We know they have extensive underground facilities and we hope to take out as much of that as possible. Two missiles on each plane have EMP weapons. They launch next to try and take out all of the electronics still operating. The remaining missiles go last and target any above ground structures still standing. Double check your firmware. We will not communicate again unless one of us discovers a problem; in that case warn the rest of us immediately. You know the codes. Good luck. Any final questions or issues?"

There were no questions. Six days later the exercise began.

Hines, talking to Clarke in private in his drab military office and matching uniform, said "Clarke, what are you doing? You are not following the exercise plan. What is this with the dummy bunker busters?"

Clarke speaking for the record, "I thought, in my best judgment, we should throw in a few curves and see if our people can deal with them."

Hines knew perfectly well something was going on. Surveillance tracked the whereabouts of every staff officer all the time. Clarke and his top computer people were unaccounted for on a number of occasions. Hines had his suspicions but decided to ignore the reports and wait to see what transpired. "We all know that Cathcart and Huber blackmail the lot of us. Did you decide to do something about it?"

Clarke, lying to the camera: "No, of course not. There would be repercussions of the most severe kind."

All of a sudden there was a blinding flash of light followed by a shock wave. The windows shattered. Both generals were knocked over and emerged cut and bruised but otherwise okay. Then there was a loud noise. A moment later there was a second slightly fainter flash of light.

Clarke, yanking a camera off the wall behind what was once Hines' desk: "Let's rip out the cameras. I assume you have swept your office for bugs, viruses, and malware on a regular basis?"

Hines replied, "Yesterday. Looks like you were tired of being blackmailed, tired of being a puppet on a string, tired of having your life ruined."

Clarke concluded, "I figure you are, too. Otherwise, you had a clue and would have investigated me. You know, as chief of staff you will be blamed. You and your family will be wiped out, if not by Cathcart, then by the Prime Minister. The last straw for me was the genetic mutation of a fifth of the world's population. If they readily committed that monstrosity, what will they do to the rest of us next time? Their paranoia only increases over time, especially now that they have messed up the lives of so many people and made lots of new enemies. This will become the norm and it will just escalate from here, same as always."

Hines had his own plan. "I'm well aware of that. Do you have a follow-up plan? I have a few necessary steps in mind."

Clarke answered, "The prime minister will want to rebuild the computer complex and run it himself. He'll want to take over where Cathcart left off. We need to capture him. When he is out of the picture, every two-bit politician in the world will want to take over the government and do the same. That's what people take as the norm these days."

Hines decided that an immediate, temporary military coup was in order. The Prime Minister would demand martial law. He would figure he couldn't trust generals and go to the next lower ranking officer he thought he could trust. Then would arrest and execute all of the generals just to be sure. As a result, Hines and Clarke knew that their senior staff would be forced to support them.

The two of them knew they had to beat the Prime Minister to it and immediately impose martial law themselves. This was quickly followed by a press release broadcast all over the internet with the cover story that terrorist forces had penetrated the Security Administration. The generals claimed that Cathcart and the Prime Minister were in hiding and they were acting on their behalf.

Meanwhile, Hines told Clarke, "We have an immediate situation to deal with and I'm delegating that to you. What is your plan?"

Clarke responded, "Cordon off the Prime Ministers' palaces and legislature buildings all over the continent. We'll tell them this is for their own protection because coordinated terrorist attacks are underway and their lives aren't safe because they are targets. Nobody goes in or out. They will all have to sign a loyalty oath to the military.

"The dummy robots and drones are about to stage their fake attack on the perimeter of the security complex. Let the Security Administration's robots engage them. I will tell my subordinates the Administration's security robots have been compromised. When they are all out in the open attacking the dummies, the planes supposedly flying cover overhead must attack and destroy the robots. We have to secure both compounds, and I have a squad of Canaille volunteers trained and ready go in and find Cathcart and Huber and place them under military arrest right away. We have to get every living occupant out of both compounds and bring them to the base hospital for so-called 'treatment.' We have to find every computer we can and pull out its memory for our examination. If it is still functioning, we turn it off, pull its memory, and destroy it. All administration survivors have to undergo 'intense' questioning. You know what I'm talking about. What we need is information about the administration's assets, computers, operations around the world, every link and connection, and the design of every piece of malware so we can neutralize their entire operation. When we're through, we blow what's left of both of these compounds along with any other Security Administration facilities anywhere in the world to smithereens."

Hines concurred, "I'm all for exposing the entire extent of their covert operations and plots to the public, so we can completely discredit the administration and the international government that sponsors and condones them. The public will be outraged, but we need their support. I know these revelations will provoke anger, generate some shock and awe. Get to it while I secure our communication channels and start spilling some of the dirt on the Administration. We need public support, but we don't want to spark mob rule."

A strong wind whistled through, followed by a low rumbling in the background.

Outside, more than 600 Administration security robots were firing laser weapons at the hapless dummies, destroying them while fighters flew around the compound at low altitude. It sounded like a swarm of mosquitos wandering into a bug zapper. In the middle of this, all of a sudden, the fighter planes started firing their laser and neutron beam weapons at the Administration robots, reducing them to charred rubble.

We catch up with Hines and Clarke about an hour later.

Hine's secretary announced, "General Hines, I have an Army Major Reilly on the phone from the Prime Minister's main palace."

Hines answered, "Hello, major, what is your situation?"

The major stated, "We have the palace surrounded. There are two helicopters with the official seal preparing to land on the roof."

The palace consisted of a large three-story white plantation style building with floor to ceiling windows, a flat roof, and a large, immaculate green yard with sparse, low shrubbery.

Hines ordered, "Shoot them down."

The major was surprised. "Pardon me, sir?"

Hines ordered again, "Shoot them down immediately, right now."

The major replied, "Yes, sir."

At the prime minister's palace, a helicopter on the roof exploded in a ball of fire. An instant later, the other helicopter above the roof also exploded into a ball of fire and crashed to the roof. The roof caught fire.

The major reported, "Sir, the palace is on fire."

Hines reinforced his commands, "Let it burn. If fire trucks come, keep them out."

The major was unsure of his orders. "Sir, there are probably hundreds of people in there."

Hines replied, "They should flee from the building on their own. Arrest them all and throw them into the brig for questioning. That includes the Prime Minister. As soon as it is safe for robots, go inside and find everyone you can and send them all to the brig as well. There are underground offices, so be sure you sweep everything thoroughly. Do you understand my orders?"

The major replied sheepishly, "Yes, sir."

Men and women were running from the palace and being rounded up by army robots and personnel. They were herded into groups to await trucks that would take them to a military jail.

Angry mobs, especially the Canaille, were gathering at government buildings all across the continent and, indeed, all around the world. The scene at the national legislature building was in view. Rioters were running around a sprawling four story elaborately ornate white building in totally uncoordinated fashion, yelling at army robots and soldiers in riot gear. Soldiers were preparing to hose them down with water cannons.

Captain Nesbit, using his watchphone, reported to Hines, "General Hines, there are thousands of rioters here. We need stiffer measures than just water cannons. Please tell me what you will authorize."

Hines replied, "Captain, belay the water cannons. Let the rioters enter the buildings. Nobody can leave the grounds again, but the rioters can enter the buildings at will."

The captain was surprised. "Sir, are you sure?"

Hines ordered, "Don't question me, captain. This is a time of national emergency. Do you understand your orders?"

The captain responded, "Yes, sir."

Clarke asked Hines, "What was that all about?"

"We have to throw the fear of God into these politicians. They have to understand the people will not willingly tolerate any more repression."

"It's a mob out of control. They will tear anybody they run across limb from limb."

"You're telling me they mean business? War is ugly and this is a war. If we stand in the way of the mob, we are at war with the people ourselves and we have lost. I think the wisest course of action is to stand out of their way for a short time until their fury is spent. When sanity starts to return little by little, we have to move in strategically and assert control. By then, people will be desperate for order and a dictatorial leader to follow, and we will be the means of providing it. They will look to us. To the Canaille, we will be leaders riding in on the white horse, and that is what their altered DNA programs them to long for. We will become their leaders. Mobs respond to anyone who senses what they want and holds up an image in front of them. The image says 'follow me and I will satisfy everything you are longing for.' If they are possessed by a single archetype at the moment, then they will follow whatever image seems to satisfy that archetype.

"It's usually a mirage brandished by a demagogue. If the immediate circumstances change, some other subconscious motif may pop up and take over their mind. Then they may quickly flee to a different demagogue with a different image. We need to find an image that will appeal to them, a realistic, attainable, lasting image that serves them. We are not demagogues."

Clarke wondered, "Won't they be appalled at what they have done when they sober up? Shouldn't we put a stop to it now?"

"Some may be appalled, or nobody could be appalled. You never know with mobs. I expect mixed feelings."

"You know we will have to genetically screen the entire world's population and quarantine anyone who has the virus or the mutated genes, so it doesn't spread any further."

Hines added, "I hope they will cooperate with us after we 'save' them, and I think they will. I would rather not do it by force."

At the legislature building, someone improvised a makeshift guillotine outside the door. Men and women were being dragged kicking and screaming out the door and forced into the guillotine to die. Bloody heads were everywhere. It was a gruesome scene. Fire started to appear from some upper floor windows. Mindless, long pent-up rage ruled the day. The unconscious mobs could not be controlled or stopped by any means.

Similar scenes were repeated all over the continent and around the world.

"You know, Clarke, I expected things to degenerate and spin out of control rapidly. A score of wannabe dictators are already springing up trying to fill the vacuum. I think I know what we have to do. Did you have any ideas yourself?"

"I'm thinking about it, but no detailed plan yet. We know we have to expose government corruption for what it really is and show the world they have no legitimacy. We know we have to act swiftly to impose order and establish the army as the only legitimate government. I will take steps to immediately dissolve the legislatures and take military control of the key government agencies and key posts and institutions.

"We have to take over the media since are already controlled and manipulated by the government. As you also know, we need to assure the loyalty of the military and purge any officer that doesn't support us. Any officer who directly benefitted from the corruption of the Administration will oppose us and want to restore the old order."

Officers were reporting from around the continent and even from some foreign capitals: Flash mobs were attacking and burning government buildings, corporate headquarters, and banks. It was unfortunate, dangerous, and deadly, but necessary to stamp out the old corruption.

Since people no longer knew how to govern themselves, some would want Hines and Clarke to become their new benevolent dictators. The generals would have to change those expectations. Unfortunately, toadies seeking their own absolute power would spring up all around them. It was another danger they had to abolish.

Ever since the virus, the entire population was subjected to genetic testing by the government. Anyone with Canaille genes, even if they were recessive, was now officially labeled as Canaille and forced to live only in designated Canaille settlements. They were forbidden to interbreed with other classes.

At least they had a lot of freedom inside our own communities. They could live harmoniously together, free of the coercion and heavy-handed treatment they suffered before. Although there were exceptions, they were mostly restricted to blue collar and routine professional jobs, but at least they were respected for the high quality of their work, which they took pride in.

Ted hated Cathcart now. "Did they catch Cathcart and Huber?" he asked.

Jenna replied, "Nobody ever found either one of them and they were never heard from again. To this day what happened to them is a mystery. People speculate about it but nobody knows. You know, some people say they contracted a mutant gene form of the virus themselves and it turned them into zombies. They say they are still alive, and from time to time they inhabit the bodies of other politicians here and there, trying to relive their past."

Leah wasn't amused. "Mom, you're scaring me."

Chipper changed the conversation, "Both of them died a long time ago. They can't hurt anyone anymore. You know, the two of them were paranoid someone would find something they could use to blackmail *them*. So, they erased their personal records, tax records, and everything else from the government and public databases. All anyone knows about them now is their public personae, memos and papers some people secretly copied, and what a few people who knew them remembered. Nobody knows much about their private lives, not even when or where they were born."

*　*　*

At Titian, the work continued at a feverish pace. Testing revealed that performance margins for the cosmic ray shielding, heat dispersal system, and magnetic radiation shields might not be adequate, so improvements to these systems were given a higher priority.

They had to start thinking about other non-technical issues. However unlikely, there was a possibility of possible primitive technology on the closest target planet, although the data was uncertain and easily dismissed. And by the time they arrived at the destination planet, existing species and the environment could evolve into something unexpected, and there would be no way to know in advance.

It was up to Thor, Michael, Osler, Forbes, Skinner, and Carson to list the possibilities and come up with guidelines, just in case, especially in the eventuality that some kind of primitive intelligence existed or was evolving, whether it be smart apes or intelligent cyborgs. Probably, there would be nothing there. The precise situation could be simple or it could be complex and unpredictable.

They all agreed on this outline of what contingencies and questions might arise if they found advanced or advancing life forms:

1. <u>Biologics</u>. Are there biological hazards? Are we and the life forms at the destination mutually poisonous? What are the geographic, climatic, and habitability zones?

2. <u>Intelligent and other life</u>: If it exists, how many different species are there? Are the creatures dimorphic or polymorphic? What is the population density and where do they live? Are they aquatic or amphibious? Do they conserve or exploit their environment and what is their overall impact on it? How advanced are they, and how are they organized? Although there are no signs of it, what if, by the time we arrive, creatures have evolved and advanced even to the point of colonizing or allying themselves with other planets in their solar system?

3. <u>Psychology</u>: What are the morals, beliefs, worldviews, philosophies, religions, and instinctive behavior patterns of higher-level multicellular life if there is any? Are there societal classes or animal sub-classes, and how do they fit in and view themselves? How primitive are they? Are they natural born hoodlums or predators and will it take a police state to control them? Are they instinctively altruistic, ethical, natural leaders or followers, power-crazed, greedy, self-absorbed, unprincipled, cruel, vindictive, individualistic, territorial, or herd animals? Are they

cooperative or antagonistic or clannish? Do their instinctive behavior patterns continue to make sense, and are there any of their behaviors it would be wise for us to adopt?

4. Moral Obligations: As the superior beings, we certainly would have a moral obligation to correct them and provide them with the goals and values they should have. How do we go about it? If there are ape-like or similar creatures with rudimentary intelligence, we would have a moral obligation to steer their evolution in the right direction.

5. Possibility of Advancement: Can they be trained or educated? Can they even understand our superior knowledge, ethics, and technological prowess? Are they sophisticated and nuanced or are they hopelessly unsophisticated? If we guide and educate them, as we would be morally obligated to do, will they use the knowledge constructively, destructively, purely instinctively, or not at all? Will they even be worthy of our enlightenment in the first place?

6. State of Society: Are there ongoing wars or catastrophes, famines, enslavement, or accepted cruelties? Are they organized planet-wide, in clans, or somewhere in between? What about ethnic or species and subspecies differences? Is life easy or consumed with hardship? Will we be forced to take sides in wars or disputes?

7. Resources: Will we compete with them for resources or can we cooperate in their extraction and conservation? Have they caused any critical shortages already?

8. Communication: Is communication even possible? Will our computers be able to translate and decipher their language or noises, history, politics, unconscious social assumptions, behavior patterns, religious beliefs, nuances of interpretation, figures of speech, historical and cultural references, unconscious knowledge, sacred values and beliefs, or deep meanings, especially if this varies between groups, subspecies, cults, and social classes? Are any kind

of understandings or agreements possible, whether local or planet-wide? Will they interpret agreements differently than what we intend? If there are disagreements, how do we correct their interpretation? Are any of their groups, clans, or tribes trustworthy, and how do we gain their trust and confidence?

9. <u>Prime Directive</u>: Above all else, our first obligation is our own survival, and our second obligation is to spread ourselves and our culture throughout the galaxy, because we are unique and special, and the universe is singularly lucky we came to be in the first place.

Chapter Six
The Super-Volcanic Period

What would people do if another large asteroid struck the planet and caused a mass extinction? Or, what if there were massive volcanic eruptions that extinguished ninety per cent of the species on the planet like there have been in the past? What if there was another "snowball planet"? How would anyone survive? Would there be anything to eat? How could anyone avoid being cooked by planet-blanketing fires or trapped under a mile of ice? How long would the emergency last and is there anything they could do to hasten a return to normal?

Invader would not be the first time some segment of the population retreated underground to avoid destruction, although it would be the most final.

How would the Blaines prepare a new cave system that would last for centuries? What would the consequences be of living in close quarters, with limited resources, facing psychological confinement, depressive lack of sunlight, crowding, and monotony? What kind of personalities would cope and what kinds would fail? Psychological factors might extinguish life as surely as the absolute cold on the surface.

The two Blaines had to find out and plan accordingly. They would be instructed by those cave dwellers who survived the super-volcano eruptions their ancestors once faced.

The first order of business was to locate the best historian, ecologist, geologist, volcanologist and other experts available to find the answers.

They recruited historian Annalee Toybee, volcanologist Toba Indy, sociologist Max Wilson, biologist Charles Mendel, psychologist Louise James, and their own director of engineering Rube Goldstein, all under a strict agreement to secrecy.

As Toybee explained it, there was a crescendo of seismic activity in an old super-volcanic caldera starting almost two years in advance. This included swarms of tremors; a rising, swelling and stretching crust that was uplifting more than six inches a year in places; ground heat three and four times normally elevated levels; more hotspots; new geysers; new geothermal vents popping up all over the area; greatly increased venting of volcanic gases, and numerous hydrothermal explosions. As this display crept into the public awareness, the government dismissed it, claiming it was just a normal variation in the geologic cycle. While this pacified most of the public, and was soon displaced by viral videos and news from elsewhere, and by everyday concerns, scandals of the day, trending internet videos, reality TV, and wonder at who would be the last one standing on Survivor Lobotomy Island. Behind the scenes, the government was stocking its private bunkers built over the years for high-ranking bureaucrats and army flag officers.

Those bunkers were originally intended for potential periods of war or insurrection, and officials assumed they would be more than adequate to protect them when the inevitable eruption occurred. The bunkers had elaborate air filtration systems, stockpiles of food, deep wells, and luxurious accommodations including movie theaters, bowling alleys, squash courts, beauty salons, fuel and generators, internet, and broadcasting studios.

With the first forceful eruption, the politicians and generals escaped into all of the bunkers at each facility, and they commandeered all of the local power from nearby fusion plants while they were still operating. They also confiscated all of the local medical and food supplies they could get their hands on, cleared grocery stores and warehouses, and took everything they thought they might be able to use in the name of 'national defense.'

The first eruptions exceeded a rare nine on the intensity scale. Even worse, the super volcano was next to a subduction zone and triggered chains of additional ordinary volcanic eruptions. The eruption was not on the equator, but close enough to affect both hemispheres.

Super volcano eruptions can potentially trigger a mini-ice age or even a full-blown ice age if a planet is primed for it, that is, if oceanic and atmospheric circulation patterns, snow and ice cover, orbital eccentricity, and other factors are tending toward an ice age anyway, or if the planet's axis is making one of its occasional excursions towards the horizontal. In these cases, the eruptions can kick start a major ice episode because of the great quantities of sulphureous ash thrown high up in the atmosphere. There will likely be earthquake swarms, tsunamis, and large-scale firestorms from superheated gases and ash. In this case, however, there were eleven years of freezing volcanic winters when no food grew, but no new ice age. Temperatures averaged 25 degrees Fahrenheit or 15 degrees Celsius below normal.

Super-volcanic eruptions can last days or months, but lasted a month in this case. Ash fall covered everything within a radius of a thousand miles, averaging six inches deep, and it was up to two thousand feet thick around the vents. It was estimated about two thousand two hundred cubic miles of ash, pumice, and rock was ejected by the super-volcano and the follow-on chain of eruptions.

Ash is composed of glass-like shards that will tear up lungs and machinery. Great quantities of smothering carbon dioxide, hydrogen sulfide and sulfur dioxide that become sulfuric acid, and hydrofluoric and hydrochloric acids are emitted. It doesn't take much imagination to know what these do to living organisms, not to mention machinery, buildings, and everything else. Wiring insulation is destroyed, creating short circuits and destroying power systems and electrical equipment. The friction from the ash creates static electricity, which leads to lightning bolts. This creates powerful electromagnetic pulses, which destroy delicate electronic circuitry. Drastic temperature drops develop at first, and well below normal temperatures can persist for up to thousands of years, returning to normal gradually during that time.

As a result of a super volcanic eruption, typically sixty to ninety-eight percent of multicellular species can be wiped out. It was estimated to be ninety percent in this case. Farmland, crops, forests, and other habitats were destroyed globally by ash, acid, firestorms, and cold. Ocean currents were disrupted and the oceans became highly acidic. Around the volcano, all life was destroyed over a five-hundred-mile radius. The food chain disruption meant mass starvation for terrestrial and oceanic creatures.

Of course, industry captains and wealthy families were warned by their advisors and by academics. They knew full well what was coming. Most of them took the warnings and potential for catastrophe seriously and started immediate survival preparations.

There were also a handful of serious preppers, some of whom were more or less ready despite the ridicule heaped upon them.

A major population bottleneck for people and for many other species resulted. It is estimated that only between five and ten percent of the population survived.

Goldstein noted that the biggest question at the time was how long would the famine last and when would the ecosystem start to stabilize? In addition, the survivors needed estimates for how long acidification would last and when would the soil be fertile again. What would grow first and what about animal life? Where would the power and fuel for heat, air filtration, and lighting come from? How long would they have to survive underground before returning to the surface? Did they need surface robots and what kind? How would they protect their filters, underground greenhouses, power plant, robots, and themselves from the lethal air? How would they recycle oxygen, carbon dioxide, and waste? How could they ensure a supply of potable water? How deep would a cave have to be for stable temperatures, and where should it be located to minimize exposure to ash and follow-on seismic activity and avoid becoming blocked? And what about protection from EMPs due to intense lightning? Could they establish hardened communication links and communicate with satellites remaining in orbit? Could they build self-cleaning steerable automatically tracking antennas with hardened electronics and underground or radio links to the antennas to make use of satellite data? Radio waves will not propagate through very thick rock, but they can propagate through thinner layers. Accessible radio repeaters could be built underground if they were near the surface, depending on the type of rock.

The Blaines' ancestors faced daunting challenges to overcome during a short year and a half to two-year window, the exact time being unknowable. At least this time they had a decade, more or less, until it all hit the fan.

The current practical choices for power were cold fusion and geothermal where it was available. Before, the only choices were geothermal or small, modular thorium reactors. Fission reactors need a cooling source. Maybe frozen temperatures above ground would work this time? The problem with cold fusion is, while viable, it's difficult to regulate power levels and runaway heat reactions leading to explosions are always possible.

Some preppers and caving groups saw a need to establish hardened communications links with each other and to share experience, knowledge, and engineering designs. Should they join together and expose what they were doing to public scrutiny? Likely not this time.

For several decades after the eruptions, some satellites continued to operate, although their orbits deteriorated, especially elongating north to south. That meant some useful weather and surface information was available for a time, and it would be available this time as well.

Mandel explained to the Blaines that designing biospheres that will last decades or longer is difficult and complex, even though scientists have been working on it for centuries and more was known now. It requires soils with complete nutrients and micronutrients, a full micro-bacterial soil culture, recycling for all nutrients, pollinators, and all kinds of other things. Some experiments had managed to maintained biospheres for decades before something went awry, but not for anything like centuries.

There was the matter of meat production as well as gardening underground in artificial light. Most caves had fish farms. They had to recycle the fish waste and keep the water sanitary and free of parasites and dangerous bacteria.

Some of their ancestors tried to maintain a zoo of domesticated animals or embryos for repopulation when conditions improved, but that was no longer applicable.

They planned to quietly obtain materials and food up front, especially since they knew governments would claim priority access. Equipment had to be adapted or modified to suit the purpose, because there wasn't time to design and build new special purpose devices. Power supplies, water purification systems, medical supplies and equipment, robots and spares, and many things other had to be procured. Most critical were irreplaceable medical supplies and devices, which could not be manufactured underground. In addition, everything had to be maintainable.

*   *   *

James explained how things unfolded. Three days after the eruptions began and the skies progressively darkened, widespread respiratory problems started to emerge. Now the public began to panic. Many tried to escape to the opposite side of the planet from the eruptions. The smarter ones just tried to get as far upwind of the eruption zone as they could. Planes and ships were stolen and hijacked right and left, including private planes and yachts. Some people desperately tried to break into caves they found out about, to force entry using dynamite, or by attempting to find and block the hidden air intakes and water sources or by any other means they could think of to blackmail the occupants to let them in. The companies and wealthy individuals that built the caves used fortified entrances and security robots to keep the public out.

Government officials called out the army, but there were only days to go and most soldiers deserted to take care of themselves and their families. Cave diaries talk about hearing explosions and battles outside, and cave dwellers were scared and worried about the desperate mob breaking into their cave and evicting or killing them, or about the roof caving in. Within a week, as food became scarce and poisoned, toxic air took its toll, and the riots and panic subsided.

The lack of sunlight and the inability to go to the surface, and the confinement, also extracted a toll. Depression, irritability, anxiety, hostility, and short-term thinking brought about strife within the cave communities. In some caves there was crowding, lack of privacy, and lack of space that had its negative effects. With people already under duress, anyone who tried to assume authority was resented and avoided, which raised the tension level even higher. Some people became quarrelsome. There were suicides and murders. Medical problems multiplied.

Just as Hyman Minsky demonstrated that stability breeds instability in economic markets, so order bred disorder in people. The petrified order mandated by limited space and resources, forced productivity, and inflexible organization combined with limited opportunities and coercion from the inevitable controlling personality types running the caves, took its toll on everyone's spirit until the unconscious erupted in protest and chaos ensued. How could they prevent that? How could they nourish the psyche or compensate for this rigidity?

After seven- or eight-years, people could make brief excursions outside the caves, but it wasn't until twenty-three years later that people could permanently start emerging from the caves to a still frigid world. By then, social organization had permanently changed. Local dialects and subcultures started to emerge. Organization and political structure became re-organized around the individual cave and mine complexes. That was the basis for new political principalities; the old boundaries were no longer respected.

Naturally, the closer to the erupting volcanoes, the more destruction there was and the more pronounced the die-off.

Adjacent areas had much different recoveries, depending on whether damage was due to lava, ash falls, pyroclastic flows, tsunamis, or other causes, and depending on the amount and kind of soil enrichment from the volcanoes.

Some small animals survived in underground boroughs. It was an unbalanced ecology. There was little diversity at first. It took a half a millennium to re-establish sufficient diversity and balance for a stable ecosystem.

Organisms migrated in from the less damaged areas; however, the change to a colder climate meant many of them would die out.

There was a succession of plant and animal cultures as old species re-established themselves, and as new species drifted, migrated, crawled, or flew in. The pace of evolution accelerated. This was regulated by the extreme cold and very gradual warming over centuries that continually shifted the climate, making all ecosystems unstable. The survivors actively cultivated and promoted new growth, but it was especially hard living for centuries.

*　　*　　*

How did governments prepare for the eruptions during the super-volcano period? Toybee explained.

When they weren't assuring the public there was no need to worry, top officials were preparing their own retreats just in case, mainly by stockpiling. But governments operate by consensus, power, and compromise, and aren't organized to do anything quickly. When the eruptions started, the officials retreated to their underground bunkers. But they lacked proper understanding of biospheres and volcanic winters, mainly because of the difficulty of distinguishing between both the correct environmental facts they knew about and the wrong-headed assumptions of their own self-serving climate propaganda, and in addition, they didn't have a complete command of all of the know-how to re-engineer machinery. Eventually the food ran out and there was nothing to replace it. The food chain was disrupted all over the planet and there was no more food to be had. Sooner rather than later, ash shards and sulfuric acid destroyed their atmospheric filtration systems. They were forced to either open the air vents or suffocate, but then the acidic air and sharp glass-like particles started to destroy their lungs and their equipment. They hadn't had time to go through all of the required permitting, impact statements, and other red tape to install underground power, so their power failed when above ground generating plants they commandeered were buried in lava or destroyed by ash and acid. As a result, they had to rely on temporary power, which soon ran out. Not many survived.

They did not die out right away. Governments are good at exacting tribute, but they produce very few material goods. So, they sent Tax5 tax collecting robots and drones to every cave and habitat they knew about. The scheme was to measure the square footage of every cave and exact a hefty real estate tax, payable in food, oxygen, and power generators. But, the machinery of the robots and drones became ground up and corroded. The drones crashed. By the time the robots reached the other caves, their lasers and neutron beams and their locomotion systems were near useless. Private cave security robots made short work of the Tax5 robots and scavenged any parts they could.

Governments used the Canaille extensively to remodel and shape their caves and mines, and to seal up any openings that would allow unfiltered air to enter, in exchange for residence. In the mad rush, no thought was given to the psychological problems of living underground in a confined space. A lot of people went crazy.

Governments also used every outlet at their disposal to ridicule the private cave builders as pathological, misguided "preppers," and dismissed them as lunatics. The major media took up this theme and did everything they could to support that view. Ridiculing the preppers became a popular public sport. Maybe the Blaines would get the same treatment!

*   *   *

Many trade-offs were already known from the caves of the super-volcano period. For example, not making the caves too big to maintain but at the same time providing open space and allowing for individual and family privacy; availability of familiar, comforting things and familiar activities including movies, libraries, educational materials, and recreational and cultural outlets; elimination of pollutants and contaminants; and waste disposal.

There were new problems such as sealing the caves and designing fail-safe giant diaphragms to maintain and control air pressure that would otherwise seep away; identifying and immediately repairing air leaks; maintaining air seals; and using robots to mine and purify new frozen air and other materials from the surface.

Most concerning was that the Blaines would have to play God, since not only was psychological screening of the utmost importance, but medical resources would be limited, so seriously unhealthy people had to be excluded.

Chapter Seven
Progress

Some people just have a way of getting whatever they want, invariably at someone else's expense. Annie was one of them, and in her experience, there was no such thing as karma.

She was talking to Conway, in his office, as she tendered her resignation. "Your shareholders and board won't be happy when they find out you are spending large sums on your colonization project. They would rather have dividends to spend now while there is still time to enjoy it. Your big deal project just reduces the bottom line and their dividends. Why are you such a stupid CEO?"

Conway was irritated. "Annie, you've been nothing but a thorn in my side since you joined this company. You're an enormous pain in the butt. The Prime Minister has this notion we will blast Invader out of its orbit and blow it up for him, and then he will be the all-time greatest ever hero ever. We're the best company to carry out that kind of project. It will give us enough profits and cover to finish the colonization effort. So, our shareholders don't need to get heartburn over it. Not only that, bombing another planet while it is still far enough away has to be a crash effort, so the money will roll in fast and furious before it all falls apart. Wouldn't you like to stay here, be the chief saleswoman, get a huge big fat commission that's more than you could ever spend? In exchange, you can just shut the hell up and quit causing me so many headaches."

Annie, expressing contempt, "What is the Prime Minister smoking this time? Doesn't he know you can't blow up a planet, let alone such a huge one?"

"What do you care? You will have more money rolling in than you could ever possibly spend. He's the one that has to sell the project to the legislature and the taxpayers, not you."

"Are you sure the Prime Minister is serious about this? I'll give you one month to see if the project goes forward and I get a big enough commission to make me happy."

"You know I have my inside contacts. The Prime Minister knows how to sell his agenda, especially when it's top-secret need-to-know basis and nobody knows enough to complain. It's the same old story you always hear about politicians: Keep the message simple (or I should say simplistic), include a grain of actual facts, and always tell everyone who will listen the same really big lie. Trick them into thinking they have a dog in the race for good measure. It's a well-known formula that's worked throughout the ages, despite the fact that everybody knows the trick. The Prime Minister is a master at it."

"And do you know why people listen to the Prime Minister and to me? It's because people believe what satisfies them emotionally, stories they think will get them what they want."

"Not everybody."

"Well, there are a few problematic morons who are stupidly curious and want to know what's really going on. They just make themselves miserable because they discover things they don't like, things that contradict what is pleasant for them to believe, and I can take advantage of that. When other people get wind of what they know and don't like it either, they try to run those morons out of town or burn them at the stake or something. Most people don't want their pleasant, emotionally satisfying biases disturbed, and they may even get violent about it."

"And you use that against them?"

"Why not? If you convince people that what you are saying is what they want to hear, they will follow you like sheep. That's why I'm so good at selling, that plus a little good old-fashioned coercion for the recalcitrant ones. I can't help it if that's the way people are."

"Yes, I know. We are all born prey according to you. So, get out of my office and go sell something. Find some prey of your own."

Annie left with a smile on her face. She was sure she could close the trap she had set for Conway, force him to give her obscene commissions on a very large project plus all the perks she could come up with. What else could he do? She was an insider with credibility who could quit and go to the media and spoil everything for Conway.

                                    *   *   *

With four years to go, Invader was starting to appear in amateur telescopes, looming ever larger. By this time, Annie had milked as much as she could from Titian, it was time she quit and hit the media circuit. Thanks to her and the increasingly visible evidence, the rumors were no longer consigned to the lunatic fringe. Belief was spreading, and more than a few people were on the verge of panic.

A month later, the Prime Minister realized the time was ripe to get out in front of the issue and become the savior. He commandeered every internet connection, radio station, TV channel, and programmable electronic billboard everywhere:

"My countrymen, do not worry about Invader. Naysayers and doubters among us want to sow unwarranted fear, unnecessary doubt. Ignore them.

"Rest assured your government has been on top of this issue for some time now. Invader is not a threat. Fear mongers among us would spread needless panic for their own nefarious purposes. We all waste our time and squander our energy with unnecessary worry.

"We have a plan to divert Invader. It poses no threat. We were always prepared and ready for the right moment. As I am speaking to you, a large fleet of nuclear bombs has been launched to the planet and will blow it up and divert it harmlessly away.

"It's time to return our focus to the important issues facing us. Folks, we have an agenda to accomplish. If we all pull together, you and I and this government will achieve great things…"

                                    *   *   *

Meanwhile, in Thor's office, Rock Peters was doing his own bargaining. "You know, Thor, as the end approaches, we will need security robots, a stockpile of food, and warm clothes for our people. I don't think we will be able to gather anywhere near enough of these necessities on our own. Perhaps you can help? I will suggest to

Reverend Franklin he should speak favorably of your efforts to send a colony elsewhere along with missionaries to spread his message of redemption. Are you in favor of that?"

Thor agreed, "If it will keep the Reverend's followers in our camp, get them behind our colonization effort, I will do my part."

"Good. I will consider that a deal."

Peters left just as Vanessa entered the office.

Vanessa greeted her husband, "Hi, Darling. Who was that?"

"Rock Peters, one of the Reverend Franklin's staff."

"I suppose he wants to be one of your astronauts."

"No, he wants food and clothes for the Reverend's flock, in exchange for supporting the mission."

Vanessa, seductively, "Can't we spend more time together? There aren't that many years left. Why can't we make the most of it? I'll make it worth your while."

"You know how important this mission is. Time is short now, and if we don't colonize, we will die out and the rest of the universe will never know we were ever here."

"I know you're here," Vanesa said trying not show her irritation. "Isn't that all that matters? Don't you think Hannah and I are more important than your project?"

"I want it to be *our* project. I was hoping you would take a bigger interest in it."

"I know dear but I could never understand and appreciate what you are doing no matter how much I want to. Please make time for the three of us. You know we love you."

"I do love you and I promise I will find as much time for you as I can. Let's have a special night tonight."

"Come home early. No late hours tonight. You don't want to neglect your loving wife, do you?"

"Promise."

Vanessa left as Michael came.

The project goals were daunting. They hoped to have six expeditionary fleets ready, each with as many as fifteen habitats with eight astronauts each plus embryos. They allowed for twenty percent death rate on the thaw-out, although with healthy volunteers it might be no more than five percent, and it also allowed for gamma ray and charged particles that get through the magnetic shields and cause a further worst case five or ten percent attrition rate. They decided *not* to make any allowance for contingencies such as poisonings, predators, and other hazards on the target planet. They calculated that a minimum of eighty-five astronauts per spacecraft with the requisite knowledge and skills must survive to create a viable colony.

For robot scouts, they planned on a minimum of one micro-probe fleet and preferably two to arrive at the new planet ahead of the habitats, one of them to continue on to the backup target planet if necessary, plus a spare, for a total of three.

For the biological cargo, they might get by with one module, but three plus a backup would be safer for a total of four.

Just in case, they considered sending three or four laser-neutron beam orbiting weapons to the two primary planets for insurance. A weapon's laser blasts a momentary hole in the atmosphere for the neutron beam to shoot through. The neutron beams kill living things while leaving all the structures standing and intact.

All of the prototypes were completed, but many of them were over the severe weight restrictions.

Michael told Thor, "I'm not sure how many spares we can send. We talked about sending some frozen rats and test plants and animals to make sure the new environment isn't toxic. We also talked about sending seeds, essential bacteria, and bioforming bacteria and plants with the biological payload. And we have to send complete libraries with all of our knowledge and culture. I don't know how much of that we can carry."

"Work on refining the list to the bare essentials," Thor replied. "How are our stockpiles coming along?"

They continued gathering power devices, booster rockets, shuttle craft, fuel, spares, cryogenic modules, and anything non-perishable they might possibly need. Much of these stockpiles were then sent up to Titian's in-orbit launch facility, along with ample string and duct tape just in case.

*   *   *

At around the same time, in the offices of the State government...

Here we go again, Zerathud thought. This idiot Brandon Blaine and his father with their ridiculous cave fetish just wouldn't stop bothering him about permits. Why did they have to show up now, with only eighteen months left until retirement? They go to his boss, they go to his boss's boss, and then he gets a lot of heat he has no need for. He'd never seen anyone so persistent in his life. Totally uncalled for and out of bounds. Usually, if someone bothered him and wanted a big rush, he got even by putting their application forms at the bottom of the pile, but that didn't work this time. He actually had to stir himself and lift a finger or two. Being a short-timer, Zerathud didn't care to deal with this kind of aggravation. It wasn't fair.

Meanwhile, in another department…

"Ms. Fiacre, how are you today?" It was the smiling face of Brandon Blaine. The Blaines were representing their project as an experimental new kind of homeless shelter where large numbers could live. "I know you realize the importance of this project and want to do your part to help the homeless. Could you possibly expedite this for us? You can make a big difference to someone who will be depending on us for shelter in the future." Fiona was flattered someone as important as Howard and Brandon Blaine had taken her into their confidence.

"Well, Mr. Blaine, you know there are rules about hearings and studies and such. I'm not sure there is a way around that," Fiona replied.

"Can't you find some exceptions in the rule book? Ways to streamline this process? I know someone as smart and caring as you are can find a way," Brandon asked.

"I will do my best to look for something. Why don't you check back with me tomorrow?"

"I look forward to it," Brandon recited pleasantly as he turned to leave.

Working the bureaucracy was a necessary nuisance and time sink, but it was important to keep cave construction on schedule.

The Blaines continued secretly stockpiling and hiding everything they thought they might need to be self-sufficient for as long as possible. It helped that their company already made a lot of what they needed.

*   *   *

Thor continued holding weekly status meetings with his key staff.

Most recently, Titian tested its prototype of the embryo preservation system; several minor glitches turned up and were being addressed. Work was proceeding on improved cryogenic techniques under other government contracts, as was work on advanced propulsion systems.

The intense, unrelenting work, along with an increasing realization that Invader was really happening, took its toll on families and friendships.

After the latest meeting, in the hallway, Evelyn Wallace said sadly, "The only time Charles and I spend together now is here at Titian. We've had to neglect the rest of our families and I do want to spend quality time with all of them before the end."

"Me, too," Renee Jenner commiserated. "I have a brother, a sister, and my parents. Maybe I can invite some of them here. I'm sure Thor would understand and agree to that."

That evening at Thor's modest house, Vanessa sensed her husband's agitation. She wanted him to relax and enjoy their evening together. "What's wrong, dear?"

"I'm worried I might be sending everyone off to die, and emergencies can happen that aren't so pleasant. I don't want to be like some type of war lord or dictator where the soldiers are inanimate game pieces, and where suffering and trauma and casualties are just numbers on a paper plan."

"Honey, they all volunteered. You told them about the dangers, didn't you?"

"Yes, but I can't help influencing them. You know the dangers are just abstract until you have to live them. They knew theoretically what they are getting into, but now it's becoming real. Some of them only see discovery, adventure, escape, or whatever else they are longing for. I just hope their reality lives up to their vision."

"Please try not to be troubled. There's still hope. You're doing your best and any of them are free to change their mind. Just keep it in front of them so they can think about it."

"I'm morally obligated to go with them and lead the mission. I don't want to be a toady general that stays in the rear. I'd better be out in front sharing their fate."

"Are you sure? You and Conway could never coexist in the same planet. You are a threat to his dominance. He will block you. I think he will fire you the instant he is sure the mission is ready to launch."

"I will still go. Won't you reconsider and we can both go on the expedition together? If we stay here, we'll die so what's to lose?"

"Dear, we discussed this and I'm just not cut out for it. I'd be too much of a liability. I just want to make the most of the time we have left together. We have plans for tonight. Why don't we enjoy ourselves?"

*   *   *

It was becoming open season on the petrified masses. All manner of demagogues, sincere and self-serving televangelists alike, politicians seeking absolute power and influence over the populace, and countless hucksters with false remedies to sell started oozing profusely from every crack and pore. Many of these opportunists were genuinely sincere and wanted to offer comfort and guidance, while many more were not.

The Rev. Franklin gained a great many new followers who found solace in his messages. He was becoming ubiquitous in the media.

"Beware! These are the days of false prophets, of usurpers of authority, of all manner of evil wolves in sheep's clothing! Keep your gaze firmly fixed on higher causes!

"We pass through this world but once. The greater tragedy is if we lose our faith, lose our principles, if we succumb to barbarity. Then we have lost ourselves, and lost our identity, for all of eternity. We must not betray ourselves. We must always ally ourselves with the Higher Purpose. We must remain people of principle. If we attain a high enough perspective, tragedy will appear less tragic; indeed, it will cement our oneness with the Devine. Pray we don't lose our way. Pray for Devine guidance.

"Always, resurrection can only follow tragedy. Will you be worthy?

"The days to come will not be our darkest days; they will be our greatest days, if we face them with courage, with determination, and with our highest principles intact.

"Will you be redeemed or convicted? Will you live the higher life or will you degenerate into darkness?

"This is the greatest test, as great as any our ancestors ever faced. Just as they proved themselves, so shall we.

"It is a dark mood that surrounds us today, but we shall not succumb. Tragedy is our source of strength. No matter what difficulties we encounter, if we lose hope, we lose ourselves. Despair does not become us.

"These are the trials by which we will define ourselves for the rest of time. Indeed, these trials will define our entire race in the annals of eternity. We shall face the enormity of our future with grace, harmony, and brotherhood. This experience, these trials and tribulations, this opportunity, will transform us and define us as a shining light for all of time if we embrace it."

Chapter Eight
Robot World

Thor, Michael, Carson, and Osler were in Thor's office discussing radiation shielding when Van Newman walked in with a companion to talk about problems with Artificial Intelligence systems and the potential catastrophe they might well create during the mission.

Michael asked, "Does everyone know Van Newman, formerly of Robot World and Robots R Us, and now part of our team?"

Newman said, "I would like to introduce you to my robot friend Professor Hydroxide. I named him that because you'll need an antacid after you deal with him for a while. He was built from left over odds and ends. You'll agree he's quite the old rust bucket. Say 'hello' to the people Professor."

"Hello people."

"You'll notice he wasn't offended at my insults. That's because I didn't teach him the concept of 'insult' and I didn't program him with an associated robot analog feeling of anger, or a foul mouth to act on that feeling. He of course does have an ego in the sense of a conscious analysis and decision center, but he wasn't given an ego in the form of a concept of pride and self-worth that have to be defended."

Dr. Osler jumped up. "Why is it a 'he'? Are the both of you a couple of male chauvinist pigs?"

"After he has irritated everybody a few times you'll want it to be a 'he.' We at Titian Space Systems strive to be politically correct at all times. I could have made it an effeminate male or a tomboy female, so I figured the former would be more acceptable."

"Just what is he good for?" Carson queried.

"He's a lab rat researchers can study. I taught him to play board games like chess and checkers. I made him a beginner. He has to learn and improve his game from his own experience. That will give me a chance to win a few games before he gets too good and beats everybody."

"If AI is so dangerous, why should I even allow that thing on the premises?" Thor asked. "You know the old saying 'To err is human but to really foul things up takes a computer.' We don't have time for screw-ups on this project, especially metallic ones."

"You see, trouble already. Why don't you ask Hydroxide to fetch you an acid neutralizer?" Newman replied. "Seriously, we will encounter things we never knew about or imagined before, so decision-making computers can make or destroy this mission. Everyone has to understand their shortcomings and how to get around them. I'm especially worried about the stay-or-abort decision when the habitats arrive at the new planet. It will be an incredibly complicated decision based on inadequate information. It must be made by computers while we astronauts are hibernating."

Thor began, "Van, can you identify these pitfalls for us and devise a strategy to avoid them?"

"The pitfalls are well-known but there is no guaranteed solution. We *can* minimize the likelihood of a critical mistake. There are three key points you should consider:

"First, no computer, or person for that matter, can be infallible. It is theoretically impossible. The mission can be destroyed by human error or computer malfunction either one.

"Second, even if perfect thinking was possible, in a practical world, time and computing power are both limited. As a result, shortcuts, called heuristics, are necessary, leading to both human and computational errors.

"Third, both people and intelligent machines must start with some basic assumptions, capabilities, and objectives or goals. In both theory and practice, intelligence can never be a clean state."

As Newman started to explain his recommendations, he unfolded a chess board he brought along and set it up on the conference table.

(Note, readers who are not interested in what can go wrong and destroy the expedition while the astronauts are hibernating and intelligent machines are making the critical decisions, are welcome to skip to the next chapter.)

*　　*　　*

First, there is a theoretical limitation to intelligence. You cannot know everything about a system from within that system. Using geometry as an example, if you have a complete set of axioms such that you can prove to be true everything which is in fact true, there will be propositions that are false that you can, nevertheless, also prove to be true. If, on the other hand, you have a set of axioms such that you cannot prove to be true propositions that are false, there will be true propositions that are impossible to prove. This has been derived from Gödel's incompleteness theorems. It applies to any system, not just geometry.

For example, in computing, there are problems that you know in advance can be computed, and there are problems that you know in advance cannot be computed, such as diverging series. Then there are other problems that you cannot know in advance if they are computable. You just have to carry out the computation to find out, which could take an infinite amount of time to do.

Similarly, in physics there is the uncertainty principle. You can know the exact position of something but not its exact momentum and vice versa. (This also applies to uncertainties of energy and time, and a few other combinations.) There are examples from other disciplines as well like the theorem that the actions of consciousness take place within the uncertainty principle. There is what I also like to call the robot uncertainty principle. A large corporation once made a study in which they concluded that every complex software system has an irreducible number of bugs. After a certain point, if you fix one bug, it will create at least one other new one. If that's true, robots can never be perfect.

Newman explained, "What this all means is that perfect knowledge is unattainable, modeling and conception will not always be possible, and both people and intelligent machines are guaranteed to make mistakes."

"I'm sure that explains my confusion," Michael said. "I will never know my own mind, but I'd like to believe the real reason is because I'm too sophisticated for my own good."

*   *   *

There is the problem of heuristics. These are shortcuts and rules of thumb that save time or deal with incomplete information. There are many kinds and they are necessary due to the insufficiency of time and computing power, or to reason with inaccurate data or unknown quantities. Some heuristics deal with limitations and necessary tradeoffs. The point is, heuristics are a practical necessity but the price of heuristics is always reduced intelligence.

With insufficient time to completely think through a problem, accuracy and thoroughness are sacrificed in favor of shortcuts and guesses. To illustrate, General Patton once famously said an adequate solution executed in time beats a perfectly solution executed too late.

In the case of computers and AI, incomplete, inaccurate, or biased training data is a similar limitation.

Heuristics include centering, that is, relying on assumptions and taking the current situation at face value, failure to study and take past history into account, and overgeneralization of the present situation ("When you have a hammer in your hand, everything looks like a nail"). It also includes use of association, analogy, rules of thumb, canned algorithms and automatic responses, inference based on experience that may or may not be applicable, substitution and substitution algorithms, and approximations and other simplifications to make problems more tractable. Further, there are various special-purpose advanced techniques (sometimes called schemas or algorithms or programs or similar), educated guesses, shortcuts of many kinds, statistical inference based on prior observation, pattern recognition, inference based on class membership, and many others. As a side note, one type of algorithm or schema are those that build and modify new schemas from existing simpler ones (think of them as the machine tools of the AI world).

Page 97

The formation of hierarchical classification systems is a major time saver. Each level of classes has presumed attributes (that is characteristics, typical behavior, and logical operations and transformations that apply). These attributes are inherited by lower classes. There may be exceptions to the rules for class membership. This is the basis for stereotyping and discrimination, and for treating people and things the same even though they aren't.

There can be many different classification systems that exist simultaneously and an object can belong to more than one of them. It can end up being quite complicated.

Items are classified based on their attributes, whether actual or inferred. Once classified, the object or person is treated as if they possess the additional attributes pertaining to the classes they belong to, which may or may not be valid.

The short cuts summarized here apply to varying extents to people, animals, and AI.

*   *   *

Meaningful action has a purpose, that is, there is the necessity for motivation, for both people and intelligent computers. Both have goals or objectives to accomplish. The dilemma is that the objectives can either be vague and general, which will maximize intelligence and the possible responses, or they can be specific and detailed which restricts the scope of vision and interpretation, and thus reducing intelligence. Motivation necessarily biases perception and leads to mistakes.

Intelligent robots are programmed to know what we want them to do, whether that's as simple as finding answers to our questions or writing a paper on some subject, or as complex as running a large factory. The goals we want a robot to carry out have been called directives or prime directives among other names.

What enforces pursuit of the "prime directives" for an AI? It should somehow measure its own effectiveness, and use that feedback to fine tune its actions in order to improve its performance. How does an AI recognize unintended consequences? For animals, the pleasure principle provides the most immediate feedback, that is the avoidance of pain (depression, physical or emotional pain, disappointment, unpleasantness, and so on) and seeking of pleasure (joy, satisfaction, satiety, and so on). The ultimate feedback is survival and reproduction. This is another large topic.

For this purpose, memories and their associated emotional charge are organized around archetypes, along with the relevant learned and innate techniques, skills, and habits. Should AI event memories, actions ("schemas" or "procedures" or other nomenclature), and results, and feedback be similarly organized around prime directives?

Further, the archetypes and directives will have hierarchical levels of subgoals, sub-procedures, associated historical memories, and so on.

For person or machine that can use reasoning to make decisions, reasoning requires the use of a model (another very broad subject). Models are necessarily simplified pictures of reality, boiled down to the relevant factors. They usually generally include the construction of new concepts and techniques, which might be built on more primitive or basic ones. They are thus subject to a number of errors, especially in new and unfamiliar situations or in cases where the information they require is not available. Construction, available components, wise selection and use, relevance, accuracy, and completeness of mental models is another major topic. It is also another potential source of serious errors. As before, there will be a multitude of models to achieve different objectives. Some of these objectives, and therefore some of the models, will conflict and cannot be applied at the same time.

Be aware that logic and math are techniques that operate on models. They are not part of, and do not operate on the real world. The world is non-logical and non-mathematical, "non" meaning 'without.' Logic and math are strictly mental tools applied to mental models, and they appear to work because the world seems to be self-consistent. The fact that the real world itself has no logic or math will be welcome news for high school students everywhere.

Logical reasoning has to operate on symbols representing the problem we are trying to deal with. Each symbol has its peculiar properties and rules of transformation. Symbols are a component of models. If you are mixing and matching different models to solve a problem, which is quite common, you may have to translate between different symbol systems, and the translation could be approximate and subject to error. It's important not to confuse the models with each other. An example is a picture or diagram versus a verbal description. This also applies to computers and computational algorithms.

Rules are also a component of models. There are many different kinds of rules, but basically, they apply to the concepts, goals, and schemas that comprise the model. There are no rules at the primal or primitive level but they are implicit in the prime directives and primal schemas. They might then appear, for example, as inhibitions or proclivities. Rules are derived during the perception, conceptualization, and modeling processes.

Finally, here are some modeling odds and ends to consider.

A feedback mechanism is necessary to test the suitability and accuracy of the models that were constructed to solve a problem. According to the scientific method, to be useful, models must make predictions so their accuracy can be verified and they can be corrected or replaced if necessary.

Always, there must be building blocks for conceptual capabilities (e.g., percepts or primitive sensory elements plus some built-in basic processing, devices, and so on), abilities and actions (such as robot arms, basic motor skills, speech particles and capabilities, various "schemas"/sequences of instructions or events), objectives and incentives that guide action (prime directives, instincts, archetypes). By starting with basic enough primitives, a great range of thought and action is possible. This necessary basic repertoire must, however, guide and constrain action, performance, and abilities. For example, it may not be possible to frame a problem or define a situation in a way that allows a solution to be developed because the optimal percepts don't exist or they are too generalized to be applicable or the specific fit to the appropriate general pattern is not recognizable.

For AI or intelligent creatures, specific goals and high-level concepts cannot exist at the lowest levels of thought, so no distinctions can be made at the lowest level between fact and fantasy, reality and make-believe, or truth and falsehood. For maximum intelligence and flexibility, low level concepts must be patterns and networks rather than hard images. This generality, by increasing capabilities and adaptability, opens the door to faulty pattern recognition and mistakes.

Finally, prime directives, instincts, archetypes, or goals will have triggers and inhibitors that turn them on and off as is appropriate to the circumstances (ignoring obsessive-compulsive aberration). For instance, eating shouldn't be 24/7, nor should it become unnecessary starvation.

In the final analysis, instincts, archetypes, and by extension, prime directives, are non-logical (which is not the same thing as illogical). They are based on ad hoc situations that arise in the course of evolution. Nor is there any guarantee they won't conflict with each other. In fact, as mentioned, opposing or contradictory instincts will definitely be present, which it is hoped won't be triggered at the same time (for instance, the simple case of fight vs. flight). Clearly, this applies to intelligent machines as well, which have to respond to a range of situations and to new and unanticipated problems.

To reiterate, goals and objectives along with their models and solutions can and will conflict, leading to disaster if not managed wisely.

One important additional consideration has to be taken into account, and that is training. It applies to both people and AI.

Training for any complex task is multidimensional and problematic. There are many sources of bias and mistakes.

Geek note (simplified for the sake of brevity), feel free to skip it: Here is but one simple example chosen from a multitude. Neural networks are a very common AI technique. There are many different kinds of neural networks with different characteristics, and numerous architectures for each kind. Suppose you want to design and train a neural network to look for a rare occurrence. For example, maybe you want to screen star systems with planets similar to Earth along with atmospheres to look for potential life, even though you don't have comprehensive data, or perhaps you want to detect cases of fraud in the use of government grant money. Neural networks are generally trained until they give the lowest error rate. In these two cases, the lowest error rate will be when the network always says there is no possibility of life on any other planets, or when it always says there are no instances of fraud ever. In order to get meaningful results, you must over-represent planets with biomarkers, or cases of known fraud, in the training data. Furthermore, these cases must equally represent the known range of biomarkers or of fraud. But, if you over-represent the rare cases you are trying to detect, the neural network will be biased and falsely detect the occurrences you are looking for.

Diagnosing rare medical conditions is an example similar to detecting fraud. Both illustrate the value of normally neglected iterative training and neural network evolution. To explain, initially, the training set will contain actual verified cases (exemplars) of fraud (or disease) on the one hand, but the non-fraud (or non-disease) exemplars will actually contain undetected cases of fraud. Thus, the training set contains errors and will lead to sub-optimal training. However, the initial version of the neural network will probably detect additional cases of fraud in the "non-fraud" exemplars. These can then be moved to the set of fraud (disease) exemplars, following which the network can be more precisely retrained, resulting in a more accurate network. Successive iterations of this process will result in a much-improved neural network.

In addition, AI machines are subject to overtraining so that they just memorize the training set. They are subject to unbalanced training sets which bias them towards particular solutions, and to other types of training errors. Networks are usually trained with historical data, but some networks can self-train in real time. In this case, they may overemphasize more recent data, but the emphasis can be adjusted. Some networks can self-test in real time.

Input data must usually be normalized and scaled (for example, reducing to values between 0 and 1, and chopping off extreme values), redundant and codependent inputs should be eliminated or combined, and other pre-processing may also be required. This is often not trivial and can be another source of mistakes.

In order to get the most accurate results, you might create an expert system to evaluate the results of running neural networks instead of relying on a simple root mean square error rate. This has its own wrinkles. Or maybe, in order to fine tune the neural network architecture, you can create a "genetic algorithm" (after fine-tuning its parameters) to try to evolve the best architecture.

This is over simplified, but you can divide neural networks into ones that create classification categories for their input cases (it turns out that slightly overlapping categories often work best, but you might prefer exclusive categories), and pattern matching types that classify input patterns into pre-defined categories (as the joke goes, animal, vegetable, mineral, or plastic). Some types of networks (e.g., back-propagation) will always give a result even when there is no correlation (false result, but good for things like speech recognition), while others (e.g., adaptive resonance theory) are unlikely to give a false result but will fail to classify some classifiable cases.

There are more sources of error such as over-training, data biases which aren't always apparent, and so on.

Architectures can become complicated for complex problems. For example, there can be networks to pre-process and post-process data, data or results of a network can be classified by another neural network and then there can be multiple networks that process these subsequent results depending on the category, and so on. The point being that in multi-faceted applications, it takes great care to produce the best AI system.

Did I succeed in scaring you half to death about the dangers of AI?

(As always, the textbook says the rest is left as an exercise to the student.)

Page 103

*　　*　　*

The heart of this analysis, according to Newman, was to determine where errors could occur in the expedition's scout, life support, and other AI robots, and to determine what can be done to detect these errors and abort or correct them when human intervention was not possible.

At a minimum, strategies and safeguards had to be developed to detect and mitigate these sources of error:

(1) The more specifically the problems the robots must solve are defined, the more precise the primitives have to be, and the less creativity the machine will be capable of. Either they can be very specific about what the machine has to accomplish, in which case the machine will be more stupid akin to an insect, or they can define the goals as a very general pattern in order to handle the unexpected, in which case the machine may well do something entirely unanticipated and possibly dangerous or fatal.

(2) Incompatible goals and models triggered by appropriate circumstances make a robot adaptable in a wider range of circumstances, but open the door to paralysis resulting from conflicts; pre-defined prioritization might help along with exploration of unintended consequences (time and data permitting), at a cost.

(3) Centering, as discussed, includes mis-evaluation of context or pre-requisite conditions.

(4) There is failure to adequately explore unintended consequences.

(5) Insufficient and inaccurate information and/or procedures and/or concepts and/or models, not knowing what to do with information, failure of an alarm to trigger, lack of resources, and similar situations; this also includes managing noisy data, eliminating redundant and codependent inputs, and improper scaling and normalization of inputs.

(6) Perceptual, conceptual, and practical limitations with resulting inadequate basic building blocks (sensory, mechanical, schematic, etc.).

Page 104

(7) Modeling limitations and resulting gaps in knowledge.

(8) The necessity to use heuristics in order to respond in real time and in order to address processing time, memory, data reliability, and other practical limitations.

(9) Pitfalls and inadequacies of pattern recognition as summarized above.

(10) Illusions and other errors of perception, of processing, and of pattern recognition.

(11) Complete and reliable data, information, and complete foresight are usually impossible.

*   *   *

Newman's mitigation strategies included the following. Titian already had experience in some of these techniques from their spacecraft and interplanetary probes.

(1) Every critical AI analysis should be computed by at least two different machines, programmed differently. If the results don't match, a third intelligence, either human or machine, makes the choice.

(2) For especially difficult problems, having multiple machines look for solutions using different models and different assumptions can pay off. Sometimes, a problem may seem insoluble using one model and approach, but become simple using a different model or set of assumptions, that is, a different paradigm.

(3) All decisions that precipitate a critical or potentially dangerous action must predict the expected outcome of that action. The results of the action must always be monitored to see if it matches the predictions (there may be some interpretation involved, a potential source of error). If the results contradict what is expected, then either corrective action must be *immediately* initiated or the action aborted and a 'plan B' implemented. Two different machines may reach the same conclusion but for different reasons. Therefore, they may make somewhat different predictions and if one machine is more accurate it becomes primary.

(4) All machines must either be self-repairing or have redundant components or have a backup. All machines should have built-in health monitoring. For example, they should have self-correcting memory, alternate power sources, continued limited functionality if the machine is degraded, and duplicate circuits that can be switched in automatically. One reason for this is the harsh space environment. Energetic charged particles, gamma ray bursts and other intense radiation, and micrometeorites will take an inevitable toll over the many decades these machines will be in space.

(6) Every robot should have a people-controlled kill switch. This means either kill everything right this instant, or finish what you are doing and then stop, or kill all thinking and analysis programs but continue to perform assigned tasks, or find an alternate way to continue if aborting the AI could also be fatal.

(7) Newman proposed a division of labor among AI's. He suggested using two classes of computers and robots. CMI93 machines, the most advanced machines available, would be used as master intelligences. These would not carry out any activity but would focus on conceptualization, modeling, problem solving. The CMI93s would have to be modified to minimize weight and energy consumption, and have improved self-correction and internal duplication, and they would all communicate with each other. Each module should have two or three sub-modules with differing directives and primitives. They would all receive inputs and data from the other robots and from people as well as from each other. Special purpose robots would be utilized for 3D manufacturing, meteorology, chemical and other analysis, and so on. These other robots could be more general and somewhat interchangeable for some of their functions, thereby minimizing how many were needed. A minimal set of interchangeable backup robots would save resources.

(8) Clearly, since basic primitives must be available for both AIs and human minds, neither of these can ever be a blank slate. One consequence is that every intelligence necessarily has its unique built-in biases and blind spots, and has actions that it is compelled to carry out. You can therefore say that every intelligent machine has its own

distinct "personality" and its own idiosyncrasies. Newman hoped that combinations of machines with different "personalities" could be used to create a useful synergy.

(9) The logic of the machines they relied upon were beyond the ability for any person to understand. Studies show that as a result, most people will happily and unquestionably follow a machine's directions. They had to resist that temptation and remember their perspective can occasionally be more illuminating than a computer's.

Besides spacecraft and habitat maintenance, safety monitoring, and advance probes, there were obvious additional uses for AI and robots upon arrival at the destination: meteorology, biology, ecology, chemical analysis, agriculture, dissecting and understanding alien ecosystems, and communication between organisms.

*   *   *

Current weekly status included a problem discovered during prototype testing of some of the habitat components, and other components that exceeded their allocated weight.

Subsystem experts including Newman were tasked with cross-training fellow astronauts.

Chapter Nine
Training

"Whoever steps onto the new planet first will be famous for the rest of time, not just on this first planet but throughout the galaxy. They won't only be known on the planets we conquer, but everywhere. I wonder which of us will have that honor," Osler questioned.

"Whoever steps onto the new planet will be the first to be eaten. The inhabitants will have telescopes and see us coming. They'll have big pots of boiling water waiting for us at our landing site," Forbes observed.

"Shut up you two!" Charles Wallace interjected. "Thor is looking for special qualities in a leader and you don't exhibit any of them. I'm the leader type in this group and I hereby delegate the first step to Forbes. He looks juicy and tender. While they're busy seasoning him the rest of us can sneak out and get a settlement started."

"I have you know I'm on a strict diet of garlic and horseradish. They wouldn't dare eat me," Forbes countered.

"They all like spicy food. Every single one of them. You won't be spared," Osler said.

Carson jumped in. "That's enough, please be serious! What if there are tech-savvy natives who don't want us carving out part of their planet and they come after us with nukes or poison or biological weapons? Suppose the dominant natives are 400-lb alpha male gorillas with 2-foot fangs and razor claws, and they don't tolerate rivals in their territory? That's what you'd better to worry about."

"Maybe we can form strategic political alliances. We have technical know-how they can use. We can exchange knowledge for materials, food, tools, or property. If we have to, we can exchange recipes, maybe offer them Forbes and a cook book," Jenner said.

Forbes interrupted, "Now you *are* getting to be annoying. You know we are thinking about sending neutron weapons to orbit the planets we colonize, just in case. If all else fails, nuclear diplomacy should work. Besides, what if the atmosphere or the native plants are poisonous? What if the planet is too toxic to live on?"

"That's why we let the lab rats out first. A rat will be famous for the first step, not you."

"Can the rats find us food and shelter? Can they inventory what materials will be available we might need and find out what's safe to eat? How do we figure out if the soil and climate suitable for the crops we want to grow?" Skinner asked.

"What if the weather is too extreme or there was a rare meteor strike or a super-volcano? What if there is a war going on and we're in the way? What if the natives just have an aggressive, territorial, and murderous disposition?" Jenner asked.

"We may have to hang out in orbit while the rats and the robots sort the situation out," Forbes said.

"But then if we have to go to the backup planet, how do we replenish our supplies and retrieve the trained rats before we leave? And then we have to worry about the risk of going back into hibernation," Osler observed.

"You know, some of those things will be determined by the advance probes, so if conditions aren't right, we will be automatically sent to the backup. We won't even be aware of that happening until we wake up," Jenner said.

*   *   *

"Ladies and gentlemen, distinguished guests and luminaries, and the rest of you who don't fit into those categories, here is my latest weekly report," Thor updated his key staff.

The highest priority was addressing a couple of habitat issues. Integrating of components that passed their unit and subsystem tests was next. They were making good progress achieving weight allowances. The power budget was tight, but they continued to make breakthroughs on miniaturization and maneuver techniques to alleviate those concerns. Maximizing propulsion efficiency was always an ongoing effort, and was proceeding as anticipated. Upgrades to production plans to make certain all components would be ready ahead of time, before social structure started to deteriorate, was another ongoing activity. Getting components to the in-orbit geosynchronous facility for final assembly and storage in plenty of time also continued. The sooner work could be transitioned to their expanded in-orbit facilities, and the more work they could transfer there, the less they had to worry about inevitable societal breakdown.

Inventing and testing the models and heuristics for the decision-making software, along with creating test scenarios for in-transit emergencies (such as shield loss and excessive radiation, air leaks, power failures, thrust failures, and different geological, ecological, biological, and other conditions they might find at the target planets), was assuming greater importance now. So far, the AI software was giving an alarming number of nonsensical analyses when confronting it with novel situations. This was no surprise, but it was difficult to predict when they might see the end of this development.

Thor was genuinely concerned about workers who would stay behind in the in-orbit geostationary facilities. He therefore started directing the augmentation of the in-orbit habitats at the geostationary facility to make them into small-scale biospheres that would last until their fusion power failed. This would be a gradual effort over a number of years.

Finally, it was time to expand the explorers' cross-training. It was time for them to start learning spacecraft engineering and operation details required for the mission in a simulated space environment. This included learning about all aspects of operations, tools and devices, including repairs, use of tools, and related activities.

*   *   *

Charles tried to be serious. "Honestly, our target planets all have lifeforms, and I'm sure microscopic life is everywhere. What substances does it produce on the new planet? What are its defenses? Will it attack us? Are we an ideal food source for it? What is our defense? Can this life produce the nutrients we need? We already found microbes in underground oceans on some moons orbiting gas giants. They use slightly different amino acids and DNA than we do. We could find just about anything where we're going."

Skinner piped in. "You can speculate all you want, but we really have no idea what we'll find. What if inheritance is based entirely on RNA mechanisms, or tPNA? Even here in this solar system, there are variations in DNA chemistries. Consuming this alien life could well be fatal for us."

"In that case, would we ourselves be poisonous or beneficial to them as food? And which kind of people do they have a taste for? Good way to get rid of troublemakers if you ask me," said Forbes.

Charles came back with, "Our new supreme ruler of the planet will decide who we feed to these monsters."

"Are you volunteering? Should we call you Mr. President or Mr. Zookeeper?"

"That's *Dr.* President," Charles corrected him.

"Van, you like to hunt. Do you think you can protect us all from those mega-monsters?"

"Piece of cake. Maybe I can be Dr. Zookeeper's right-hand man."

Osler imagined, "It would be fun to come back and tell all our nieces and nephews and grandchildren bedtime stories about all the two hundred-foot monsters chasing each other all over the planet, the hundred-foot snakes, the flying predator birds that are all jaws and stomachs, the man-eating plants with suction systems, and how we narrowly escaped from them all."

"Since we can't do that, I suppose we'll just have to make up some stories for now."

Carson interrupted in. "Alright, enough speculation. We have serious work to do."

"Spoil sport. You're buying lunch."

Their work was all-consuming. They had little time for family. Was it worth it? What if the mission wasn't ready in time and had to be canceled? How could they go back and spend that lost time with spouses, children, brothers and sisters, parents, nieces and nephews? Time was measured and precious now. Would they come to resent their dedication?

It all weighed on Forbes's mind.

Jenner could tell, and she empathized. "I know how you feel. For me it's just my sister and me and that's all. I will spend time with her whenever I can. At least, she is proud of me. She thinks this is a noble mission. You keep bringing this up. What gives?"

"I've decided to drop out of the program. There are so many unknowns, I just think it's too much of a gamble. Besides, geology has lost its meaning for me. I used to like the field work and I liked looking for analogs on other worlds, but it just doesn't excite me anymore. I want to spend more time with my family. You have your science and adventure to keep you going."

Jenner was shocked, even though she had sensed that something like this might be coming. "But we've been together more than eight years now. This is a future we can have together, and I don't want to die with this planet. I want something to look forward to, don't you?"

Forbes concluded the conversation, "I'm sorry, really. I think I it's not worth being part of this anymore."

*　*　*

Later, at Thor's house, Vanessa was troubled by what others in the media were saying. "Dear, don't you think all of that money you're spending on this space expedition should be used to build caves to save people, you know, like during the super-volcano? I mean, you might only save a few hundred people, but tens of thousands could live for decades in a big cave."

"If the money wasn't going into the mission, Titian would just be spending it on executive bonuses, share buy-backs and dividends. It wouldn't build caves or do anyone any good."

"But then people could use the dividends to have fun, like Annie Kolar keeps telling everyone."

"I suppose some big shareholders could live it up like she claims, but then nobody would be saved and our culture would die."

Thor knew this was a losing battle. "I do think about us. You know you are the most important person in my life. Maybe we can snuggle up and watch a movie together tonight."

"That would make me happy."

Would you, or the average person, join a mob or loot a store if there weren't food and necessities to go around and you were desperate enough?

Would you, or the average person, continue to work more than you had to if there was no future to build for? People who could abandoned their jobs, including police and military.

What happens when more people find out food, cars, clothing, and everything else they use isn't being produced anymore because there is a huge shortage of workers, and everywhere you look someone is trying to steal what's left? What happens when utility and service workers quit and water, electricity, roads, and every other service becomes unpredictable? People have long since lost the skill of self-reliance.

For the Blaines and for Titian, how would they obtain the supplies and materials they needed when the mines and factories were shutting down and workers became unreliable? How could they protect themselves when people become frustrated and hungry and angry and begin to sabotage offices and businesses? Of course, Titian enlarged their in-orbit stations and sent everything they could there when they could, and the Blaines built secret stockpiles, but could they keep them hidden and safe, and what did they forget?

It was already starting. Prices were jumping. In addition, Hughes and other companies were trying to raid Titian's remaining fusion, biosphere, and other technical experts. Retention was an issue. All of this was foreseen, but the extent, timing, and sequence of events was impossible to predict. The race was on! It was every man for himself.

Many of the wealthy already had private bunkers. Most waited until the last minute to stock them, and few had a systematic plan. Many realized, too late, that their bunkers were too small and limited, especially since most only anticipated temporary stays during emergencies. That added to the panic and chaos.

Millions were searching every spot and source to find the secret bunkers, the private caves, the warehouses and the stockpiles of goods, including government stockpiles. All were prone to seizure and theft. None were safe. There was a shortage of robot guards, not to mention that the obvious presence of guards and surveillance was a dead giveaway. Anyone who lacked the foresight to obtain guard robots in advance was out of luck.

Titian's space elevator complexes made it reasonably economical to stockpile supplies in orbit, beyond the reach of competitors, mobs, and governments, but these complexes were so critical they had to be protected and maintained to the very end. Furthermore, the handful of Titian's top experts were committed to the astronaut corps and so wouldn't be tempted by other offers.

There were two space elevator complexes controlled by Titian. They allowed for payloads of up to nineteen and a half tons to be placed into orbit at any point on the ribbon including geosynchronous orbit. The primary complex was located atop a mountain at the equator. It had five dual ribbons extending to an altitude of sixty-five thousand miles with counterweights at the top of each dual ribbon.

The backup facility consisted of two dual ribbons, each extending from a large mobile platform at sea. Protecting it from pirates and saboteurs was problematic when things started to break down.

There were usually at least one or two of these ribbons being repaired. Their extensions into space were all vulnerable to being struck by errant satellites, meteorites, space debris, and other hazards, along with vulnerability to storms and weather-related disruptions. Spacecraft in geosynchronous orbits attempted to divert space debris with laser devices, and the platforms at sea could move in a limited area, but that wasn't always successful in preventing damage.

Climbers ascended the ribbons with their payloads, driven by laser beams impinging on their large downward-aimed mirrors. The mirrors had changeable radii in order to focus the laser beams into a parallel reflection from different altitudes. Ascent to geosynchronous orbit, one in which the satellite or payload hovered over the same geographic spot, took four and a half days.

These space elevators were by far the most economical way to place payloads into orbit. The cost was a small fraction of the expense of using rockets or any other means. The complexes were built, maintained, and operated under government contract by Titian Space Systems, but the government retained ownership. During the panic period, Titian seized control from the government which was distracted with more pressing problems.

Titian was the largest aerospace contractor in the world, in part because it had bought out all of its major competitors or driven them out of existence with its overwhelming political influence and its economies of scale. It had facilities throughout the continent, but the main complex was massive. It was located along the ocean at around twenty degrees latitude. The location was advantageous for launching rockets and shuttles into space. These launches were becoming less and less frequent now. They only made sense for especially large payloads. Space elevators were so much cheaper they were exclusively used for payloads below twenty tons.

The major exception to this was placing astronauts into orbit. This was always via shuttle. Space elevators extended through radiation belts that could be crippling or fatal for people, given the relative slowness of the ascent and the length of time people would be exposed to the intense radiation.

Shuttle and rocket launches were always carried out under contract to private companies like Titian. Titian maintained shuttle launch facilities and runways at its main complex along with its own fleet of company-owned shuttles. Conway's and Thor's offices were also located there.

Titian's biggest asset was its massive spacecraft assembly, maintenance, and launch complex in geosynchronous orbit, stationary on the same longitude as its headquarters. This facility was built up over decades and at great expense. Nevertheless, it was highly profitable because it allowed Titian to undertake complex missions no other company could carry out. That included sending sophisticated exploratory probes to other star systems. Components were sent into geostationary orbit using the space elevator, and then drifted to the Titian complex. Crews spent rotating six-month shifts there. Even with artificial gravity in a rotating crew habitat, by the end of their stint the crew's muscles and bones atrophied to the point they needed rehabilitation when they returned home.

The large geosynchronous complex was easily seen as a conspicuous, stationary blob of light in the sky from a third of the planet's surface. It had a wheel and axle architecture. At the center was a six-spoked spinning wheel. Up to two hundred and twenty-four crew members and staff slept, ate and relaxed in the perimeter of the wheel under an average of half a gravity. The periphery also contained medical, sanitary, and other rooms. It was rather cramped and basic. To get to the non-rotating zero gravity working areas, crew members had to climb to the central hub of the wheel and proceed through either the upper or lower air lock. Much of the work was handled by robots, directed by the crew.

The lower axle pointed south. It contained labs, machinery and service stations, machine shops, and fabrication rooms. Just below the rotating wheel eight elongated cylindrical tanks stuck out from the axle. Two of these contained heated liquid water, two contained compressed nitrogen, and the rest contained compressed oxygen. Below that, six large storage rooms shaped like truncated pyramids radiated out from the axle, used to store parts, spares, raw materials, and fabricated components. Below that, eight cylindrical tanks fanned out lengthwise from the axle, used to refuel docking spacecraft. Finally, at the bottom of the axle, eight passages branched out like wheel-less spokes. There was a docking facility at the end of each spoke. Six of these were used for shuttles and ferry ships servicing the complex. The other two docks were used by the dedicated ferries that shuttled parts and fuel between different areas of the complex. A large spherical module extending south from the end of the axle contained the fusion power plant and fuel that supported the complex. A communication antenna farm bristled out from the sphere.

The rotating crew quarters wheel acted like a gyroscope to stabilize the orientation (attitude) of the complex. While it provided an average of half a gravity of force at the periphery, this varied as the electric motors adjusted the rotation rate for maximum stability. To balance the complex, fuel, liquefied gas, and water were transferred within and between tanks, thus helping to conserve fuel use for the attitude control thrusters.

The outside surface of the wheel was lined with solar cells to provide a small amount of emergency backup power.

The northern axle contained the assembly and final fabrication features. Just north and nearest the rotating wheel, eight special facilities radiated outward, four rectangular storage rooms and four configurable assembly harnesses with cranes. Farther out, eight cylindrical fuel tanks branched out lengthwise from the axle. Next were six fusion power assembly and fuel storage appendages. Finally, at the end of the north axle, eight spokes radiated outward. Satellites, rockets, and spacecraft being assembled and readied for launch could be docked and built up at the ends of these spokes.

The inside of the complex was Spartan and basic, with neatly routed but exposed pipes and wiring harnesses, and with computers and machinery bolted in place everywhere. Numerous airlocks throughout the complex would automatically close in case of an air leak, fire, or other emergency.

To accommodate the colonization mission, the north axle was being doubled in length and capacity, with all of the storage rooms, assembly harnesses, cranes, tanks, fusion assembly complexes, and assembly spokes duplicated. A relatively small modular thruster with a conical nozzle at the end of the north axle was used to dampen north-south orbital drift; this would have to be relocated to the new end of the axle.

*   *   *

It was time for Thor's latest weekly briefing.

They were back on track with the habitat module problems. Overall, however, they were still two weeks behind their master schedule. Nothing like hard deadlines to keep everyone up at night. The AI models still didn't correctly handle unexpected scenarios that were outside their training. They were also too slow in conceptualizing and analyzing those unfamiliar situations.

Propulsion modules and spares were well into production.

*   *   *

At Blaine Industries headquarters, Brandon reported they were trying to buy additional mining robots and spare parts, which were backordered and becoming harder to obtain. They were also trying to buy additional tunnel boring machines to extend caves and mining shafts. Customized changes were being made to them to minimize underground pollution and to avoid venting toxic gases. Blaine Industries didn't have any manufacturing capability for highly advanced robots, and couldn't easily get the components and materials to build them. The demand was beginning to exceed the supply.

Several of the mining robots would have to be able to operate on the surface in near-absolute zero temperatures. They would have to be custom modified from existing designs, a difficult proposition. Only a few companies had the expertise to build them. Rube Goldstein calculated that taking the planet's internal heat into account, the surface temperature should drop to between around minus three hundred seventy degrees and minus three hundred eighty degrees Fahrenheit.

Blaine did make domestic and utility robots, but lacked the capability, the expertise, or the materials that go into highly sophisticated designs. Their engineering department was investigating adaptations to their robot line to enable routine mining and cave maintenance chores. They were also looking into strategic acquisitions.

Obtaining the best seeds, microbial soil cultures, and soil amendments for the poor underground cave soil was also becoming highly competitive. Titian also wanted a collection of hardy seeds that tolerated a wide range of soils and climates. For this, they were in competition with Titian and Hughes. Blaine had a nursery division and were breeding special new varieties. Titian asked to be one of Blaine's priority customers. Blaine and Titian both were trying to get access to old seeds in seed banks that came from glacial ages and other extreme conditions they could then develop, but with little success. They wondered, what's the point of a seed bank if you can't grow them again when you need them? Food and pharmaceutical preservation methods were also a major push. They expanded their preservation warehouse facilities and made their expertise available to others, at a profit of course.

For Blaine, protein sources were another concern and the traditional underground method was fish farming. To support ten thousand people would require two hundred thirty acres for recirculation aquaculture systems. There were specially bred fish suitable for this purpose that fed on phytoplankton and weeds. The ponds needed de-nitrogenation and the wastewater could be recycled through underground aquifers, filtered through clay.

Another two hundred fifty underground acres at a minimum was needed to raise crops using intensive methods, plus the artificial lighting and power consumption to go with it. Until food cycles were established and also for emergencies, they needed equipment to remove CO_2 from the air and replenish O_2. Blaine didn't manufacture any of that.

Brandon reported an additional problem. The Chang family, who were the owners of the PolySeed Corporation, were building their own cave. Even though they belonged to the consortium, they made offers to some of Blaine's key agriculturists, mining engineers, plant disease specialists, nutritionists, biosphere experts, and civil engineers. PolySeed's normal approach was to create hardy chemical-resistant plants and then use herbicides to kill off the weeds. The problem was, they would poison themselves if they tried that underground, so they were stealing Blaine's people to find out other ways to do it.

*   *   *

Thor had barely begun a weekly meeting when Annie burst into the room while he was talking to Michael.

"Where is my fat commission from your subcontracts? I haven't seen one red shekel yet. And you can just shut up, Michael, I'm talking to Thor."

"You don't work for us anymore," Thor responded. "You quit, remember? And how did you get in here past security?"

"None of your business. I originated some of those subcontracts so I'm still entitled."

"So why aren't you talking to Conway about it? That's not my department."

"He's not available, so that means it's up to you to convince him. I need more money and it can't wait. I'm sure you can find other accounts to pay me from."

"You don't belong here and we have business to attend to, so please leave."

"If you don't want to help me, I'll badmouth you and your precious mission on every TV and internet appearance from here to eternity. Are you clear about that? You have one week to come up with something I like."

Thor pressed the button to summon a security robot.

The Prime Minister was addressing the nation:

"Friends and countrymen, our adversaries sow needless fear and unnecessary doubt. Rest assured your government has focused its attention on this issue. We have seen to it that Invader will not threaten us. It is time for us all to turn our full attention to the business of this country. We waste our time and squander our energy with needless worry by listening to these self-serving fear mongers."

The majority of people were still absorbed in their day-to-day business and mostly ignored Invader. However, enough took it seriously that it was starting to have an effect on the economy and the popular culture.

Some who had savings listened to Annie Kolar, quitting their jobs and pursuing the good life. Some students were just starting to see no point in preparing for a future career and dropped out of school. A few took out the largest, longest-term loans they could get, figuring they could have fun now and at some point, they would stop making payments because it wouldn't matter anymore.

Because of exploding credit, increasing demand, fewer workers, and resulting production bottlenecks, prices started to rise noticeably faster, especially for luxury goods.

* * *

At Blaine Industries headquarters, Brandon gave a status briefing to his father. "Dad, I maxed out the company's credit and made the payment terms as long as possible. Both long term bonds and loans. Long term credit is just starting to dry up. We are using the proceeds for our cave complex. I'm having a problem getting self-contained CO_2 recycling equipment and high-quality surface mining robots. I'm continuing to stockpile day-to-day necessities including entertainment, libraries, things like fitness equipment, and everything else you can think of including quality-of-life items."

"Good. Please make sure it's all hidden in a safe place, in unpublicized locations, and well-guarded."

*　　*　　*

As Invader drew ever closer and became a starry fixture in the sky, moods changed. YOLO (you only live once) was giving way to worry, depression, desperation, resignation, lethargy, and anger.

At the Kolar house, Annie was feeling it, too, and taking it out on her husband Maynard.

"I'm working as hard as I can, educating people, helping people, giving talks, getting interviewed, being an internet celebrity, making money. And what are you doing? Just sitting on your butt 24/7. You are worthless as far as I'm concerned. You don't do anything for me."

Maynard tried to deflect her groundless rage. "But I have a job as an economist so I can buy you things you want. I work hard. I'm exhausted."

"I know better and I'm always right. Who needs economists these days? Who cares about economics when the world is ending and everything is circling the bowl?"

"A lot of people appreciate what I do."

"Name one. You can't can you?"

"I build econometric models that forecast the future. People want that."

Annie, contemptuously, "You are seriously deluded. You're such a loser. You don't even own a business. You're not an executive. You're just a plain economist, nothing better. What use is that? You don't even try. You just sit around poking a keyboard day and night. At home. At work."

"It's a profession. It's not like I'm a greeter in a department store."

"What kind of profession is that? Where are your speaking fees? Nobody wants to hear you talk! Where are your royalties? You just publish stupid articles about your worthless models nobody reads.

And what kind of money do you get for it? Hardly anything! You just waste your time when you could be making more money doing something else. What a loser!

"And where is my car? I told you I wanted a more expensive luxury car, and what about the jewelry I told you I wanted?"

"But I bought you a luxury car. And a lot of very expensive jewelry…"

"What a joke. You're a joke. I told you what I wanted and you bought me something else. And I don't like any of the jewelry. It's too small and it doesn't look good. You are a pathetic excuse for a man."

"But it was what you said you wanted..."

Annie shouted, "Just shut up. I'm tired of you. I've had enough of you and your lip. Get out of here!"

She walked away, fuming.

A week later, Annie was on television, again, speaking to a studio audience. She was now a regular guest.

Annie had a message a lot of people wanted to hear. She became a very popular speaker, in great demand. "This is your life here and now! Are you enjoying it? Are you doing what you want? Live it to the max, why are you waiting? Your life is slipping away! I'm here to tell you now is your time. Pull out all the stops. You have nothing to lose! Make a list, all of the things you ever thought you wanted to do, everything you wanted to experience. Prioritize your list. For each wish, look to see, what do you need and where you can get the money. When can you fit it in? How can you fit it in? What is stopping you? What are your obstacles? Find a way to overcome the obstacles. Be determined. Make a plan. Don't wait. What can you have right now? Why wait until later? There may not be a later! Be determined, and you will find a way..."

*   *   *

Elsewhere, in some bar somewhere, it's all a blur…

Zerathud, a short, overweight, sloppily dressed balding man in his 50s, slurring his words, said, "Hey, Jimmy, let's have another round, celebrate my retirement."

Jimmy, a wiry greying six-footer, also slurring his words, said, "You just ordered another round."

"Oh, yeah, I forgot," Zerathud responded.

"My damn wife is cheating on me with my coworker Sandy. He lives down the street," Jimmy said.

"How do you know?"

"Because I called her. Her phone was busy. Then I call Sandy. His phone was busy, too. So, they had to be talking to each other and cheating together."

"Screw her. Let's have another round."

"Shut up, your wife left you twenty years ago."

"Best thing what ever happen' to me." Zerathud was now certain of that.

"That's not what you said then."

"I want me one o' them broads from that model search show. Beautiful women."

Jim, mocking: "Why would they talk to you? You're too ugly."

"You ain't no prize yourself."

"No sober woman ain't never lookin' at you."

Zerathud, turning green, said, "I'm going to throw up."

"Better head for the men's room."

"Don't think I can find it."

"Then go outside and throw up. Am I gonna have to drive you home again?"

"Looks like it."

"Pay the tab and go outside. Where are we, anyway"

"Don't know, either, but how about tomorrow again, same place, same time, wherever place this is?"

"Sure."

*   *   *

"Ladies and gentlemen, I would like to report on our current status. Last time, I thought a few of you deserved an academy award for your detail reports and I apologize for failing to provide one." It was time for Thor's next weekly briefing.

They were making up time with the habitat modules by combining prototype testing and integration as much as possible. This was a somewhat dangerous thing to do, and not a shortcut they wanted to take, so they had to proceed with it carefully. It was too easy to miss a problem or to skip a crucial test. If they missed a problem at this stage, they were dead as in the project is over. They put a couple of extra test engineers on it.

The three biology payloads had been successfully launched to each of the two primary target planets and were on their way. Telemetry indicated everything was going according to plan on all six vehicles.

They were now sending all of the spares they thought they might need that they could lay their hands on up the space elevators.

The explorers physical training started now, including water and land survival skills.

*   *   *

At the Hurlock's house in the Canaille settlement, Chipper reported, "Hon, Mr. Hughes offered me a job designing the water system for his underground retreat. He promised me a place in his habitat if there is a disaster." Chipper was a former civil engineer, specializing in water quality, before he became a science teacher.

Jenna asked, "Will you take it?"

"No, he didn't offer a space for the rest of you. I don't think he likes Canaille. You know I would never go without my family."

"Why don't you take it anyway. Maybe he will change his mind. It's a secure job and there aren't a lot of them these days. I'm not even sure about my own teaching position, so many children are dropping out of school. There isn't much certainty anymore. Make yourself indispensable."

Page 125

"You're right. I won't get a better offer."

Chipper always felt responsible for his family. Since all of them were naturally drawn to the Rev. Francis, shouldn't they just have faith? Shouldn't that be enough? Things were becoming more and more confusing.

"Didn't we talk about a family day with the kids today?" Chipper said.

"I told the kids we would go to the park and eat some ice cream. Better now while we can, because it won't be long before the parks are full of homeless with no means of support and nowhere to go, and they will trash the place."

There was a lot of noise blaring from the public square next to the park at the center of town. The Hurlocks wandered over to see what the fuss was about.

On the way, they passed some newly homeless addicts and people who recently lost their jobs. There were more and more of them, people who decided there was no future to look forward to and gave up on life.

There was a couple living under a plastic sheet laid over clotheslines stretched between trees, their trash and meager possessions strewn about them. There was a filthy man huddled in a makeshift shelter, a couple of old mattresses suspended over a stack of cardboard boxes.

There were transients just sitting about, oblivious to the weather, swallowing and snorting pain killers and other drugs. Some had sacks of stolen goods and government payment cards to trade for more drugs; some of the women traded their bodies for drugs.

It was fall. There were families in tents, poor people who lost their jobs and couldn't quite get by on their government welfare cards, even when the stores had goods to sell. One man was complaining to a woman, "I'm so tired of this. No running water, no toilet and having to hunt for public restrooms, blankets freezing to the ground at night, no stove to heat food. I get so depressed. It takes a big toll on my self-esteem. I can't go on much longer like this."

Leah was disturbed. "Daddy, why are there so many now?"

Chipper tried to soothe her. "Times are getting tougher. Jobs are harder to find. But don't worry. Daddy has a good job. We will be fine, not like these people. Let's hurry past and see what's going on in the square."

Most of the unfortunates were just hanging around. A few were listening to the speaker along with fifty or a hundred others. It was David James, a preacher just entering the public awareness, fishing for followers.

"Invader is not an accident. Its inhabitants brought it here for a reason. They are here to harvest the worthy and deserving among us. Will you be saved? This need not be a disaster for you. It is your stepping stone to a better life, an infinite future. The highest authorities on Invader have contacted me to be their conduit, their voice, to convey their message. They summon us to go on to the next step of perfection. I can promise you, we have their guarantee a better life waits for those bold enough to seize the opportunity..."

A seductive message, especially for Canaille. Chipper had to keep reminding himself he was a disciple of the Reverend Franklin, not this newcomer.

"Daddy, I want to go to Invader. What will it be like there? Is it a good place?" Leah was hooked already. She didn't want to become like the people in the park. Ted wanted to go to Invader, too. "Let's all go, together. I'm scared."

Meanwhile, Jenna was becoming quietly mesmerized.

Chipper knew they needed to go home; it was dangerous to listen to this. "He doesn't know anything. We better not listen to him. It's time to leave."

*   *   *

At Thor's house Vanessa brought up an old subject. "Do you have to spend so much time at the office? You're a stranger in your own home. Can't you at least bring work home to do, especially on the weekends?"

"I'll see what I can do. I have to oversee everything and a lot of people depend on me now."

"You know you can do your meetings over your phone."

"I will do more of that."

"Won't you please reconsider going into space?"

"I think about that, but I'm committed to seeing this mission through to a successful conclusion."

"My gosh, that's just like your father. I know how much you admired him and wanted to be like him, but you are your own man now. You are not your father."

"There are eerie similarities though, aren't there? He sailed a primitive raft across a large ocean to a new continent to show it could be done. We're sending a new kind of ship across the vastness of space to a new solar system. What challenge could be greater?"

"You're hopeless! Your father came back from his exploration. It wasn't a one-way ticket, and it didn't take a lifetime.

"You don't have to go. You're your own man and you have nothing to prove. Your father would be proud of what you've accomplished already. Would you leave your wife and daughter then?"

"I was hoping you and Hannah will change your minds and come with me. I can find a place for you on the mission. Hannah is grown, almost out of college. We can help our race to prosper somewhere else, all of us, together."

"What about Conway?"

"We have a plan for him."

Thor was not really as certain about going as he let on, even though he thought it was the right thing to do. At least, he kept his fingers crossed.

The Prime Minister was addressing the people yet again:

"Tonight, we gather to affirm the greatness of our nation. Our latest calculations show that Invader may still pose some slight threat to our planet, even after we sent our rockets there. There is no cause for concern. When the possibility of a threat materialized a few years back your government undertook contingency planning just in case. At that time, your government in its foresight contracted to prepare for a space mission to Invader to alter its course and blow it up should the need arise. As a safeguard, we have prepared a second, insurance mission to the planet, to finish altering its course and blowing it up. Preparations are completed and we are now taking immediate action. Any possible remaining threat will be eradicated. I am pleased to announce that Flash Packard, the national hero and astronaut, has volunteered to go on this special mission to make certain it arrives flawlessly at its destination and then fully accomplishes its purpose. We are planning special celebrations to mark the launch of this historic event…

"There are complaints that mortgages and long-term loans are regularly refused by financial establishments. Demand for long-term government and corporate bonds is also drying up and interest rates have increased. I want to assure you that your government is addressing this problem. As of today, all of your government housing agencies and authorities are cooperating to provide affordable mortgages with liquidity supplied by the central bank. This is a temporary measure which can be phased out soon."

People were becoming ever more confused. Governments and major media were still insisting the threat from Invader was negligible and overstated, but at the same time respected professors, alternative news sources, and tabloids were shouting that a disaster was imminent.

Some institutions were becoming wise to the fact that people and businesses were taking out loans with the intent of never paying them back. Long-term money was drying up, although short term loans were still available with suitable collateral. Mortgages were nearly impossible to obtain now, at the same time demand for high-end housing was skyrocketing.

More and more people were dropping out of the labor force and out of school, leading to lost production, low productivity, and spot shortages. Prices of many necessities and of luxury goods alike were skyrocketing as a result. However, with credit starting to dry up, other prices, mainly for non-necessities people no longer wanted, plateaued and then started dropping. The government was now stepping into the breach with the central bank actively pushing newly printed money onto financial institutions which, however, still found it wise not to lend the new money. As a consequence, the government decided to start providing its own low-cost loans for home equity, cars, businesses, education, and even some personal loans to fill the void.

Some professions, especially teachers, were getting laid off now. Suicides were increasing. Drug addiction, alcoholism, crime and homelessness were on the rise. Police and military personnel, tired of dealing with the increasing lawlessness, quit and deserted, making the problem worse. Public safety was becoming a major headache.

*   *   *

Blaine Industries long since maxed out its credit, which had now dried up. They could only get short-term money for day-to-day expenses. They spent the money they borrowed as fast as they could, anticipating shortages and inflation. This including stockpiling extra food, clothing, and other essentials to use for barter when the time came.

Beyond that, they relied on profits from day-to-day operations to see them through.

They had to maintain tight financial controls now and jettison any product line that wasn't turning a profit. There was no time to turn around unprofitable lines and no time for patience.

*   *   *

Meanwhile at the Hurlock's house in the Canaille settlement…

"Mom, why can't I have a hamburger and fries? It's been forever. Why do we always have peanut butter and jelly? I'm sick of peanut butter!" Ted scowled and pushed his plate away.

"Prices keep going up, dear. We can't afford hamburger anymore. Would you like some mac and cheese?" Jenna didn't know what else to do.

"I'm sick of mac and cheese, too! Can I go out to play?" Ted was ready to scream but he knew better.

"Go ahead but be careful. Play with friends and stay away from strangers." Jenna knew it was time to do something to make healthy food affordable again, like plant a garden. She would talk to Chipper about it later.

Chipper agreed. He started hunting for cheap seeds and compost. It would be a large, all-natural, highly nutritious organic vegetable garden with no fertilizers, no pesticides, no chemicals, nothing but natural ingredients. It had to be. Even if they wanted some, fertilizers, pesticides, and plant food were unobtainable.

The outdoors, the exercise of hoeing stubborn weeds, the digging and sifting, the contact with mother earth wouldn't hurt, either.

*　*　*

"Respected colleagues, here is this week's report on our current activities," Thor intoned. It was time for another weekly status meeting.

They were finally ready to go to production on the habitats. Van Newman was teaching the intricacies of working with and using advanced computers, especially intelligent ones.

Meanwhile, Conway was in his office talking on his speaker phone.

"Yes, Mr. Prime Minister, I understand you are in a difficult position on this. From our interplanetary probes we calculate that Invader was slightly nudged from its trajectory but not enough to miss the inner solar system. Our orbital mechanics department is recommending a third mission to finish the job."

Conway somehow managed to present this spiel with a straight face. The Prime Minister was fully committed and in a bind. He had no choice in the matter. Conway figured the Prime Minister's only alternatives were to fund more missions or to commit political suicide by admitting he made a mistake and misled the people.

"Well then, why not turn this to your advantage. Perhaps you can use it to demonstrate that you are fully up on the situation and sparing no effort to defeat the greatest problem our society has ever faced. You will soon be the greatest hero in the history of the world. You and your descendants will have carte blanche. You will become a dynasty for all of eternity."

(Pause) "Certainly, Mr. Prime Minister. As you know, Titian took the precaution of building a fleet of the new generation of more powerful rockets. We can be prepared for another launch in a matter of weeks."

(Pause) "As you wish, sir. We will proceed immediately."

Conway turned to his secretary. "Get Annie on the phone. Tell her if she can manage to keep her big trap shut for the next year and wants to come back to work for us again, she is in for another big fat commission."

*   *   *

In a luxury hotel suite somewhere…

"I'm worth billions you know." Peter, a tort lawyer, was talking to Annie.

Annie, feigning surprise, said, "Really, I had no idea you were that successful. I knew you sued large corporations."

Peter continued, "Drug companies. Easy pickings. I advertise all over the internet and on TV, and get hundreds of clients. Look, I have two houses, one in the city and one at a resort. Both mansions. I have three expensive luxury cars. Money in the bank. You know, I believe what you say. None of it will do me any good a few short years from now. May as well spend it. All of it. I'm divorced, my kids are grown, and in a few years, they won't need my money, either. It makes no sense to hold anything back. I figured you can help me with that. You can help me decide what to do."

Annie, her eyes nearly as big as dinner plates, said, "Of course I would be happy to help. You know I'm an expert."

Peter, looking out the window, observed, "Looks like a storm coming up."

"Yes. I heard a prediction for six to eight inches tonight. Are you ready for that..."

The next morning…

"Peter, honey. Does this mean I'm your girlfriend now?"

"I would like that."

"Then we are inseparable now." Annie confirmed it in her most convincing voice.

Four days later, Annie was on a promotional tour in another city, in her hotel room, this time a standard room.

"It is so nice to see you again, Andy. Nice of you to come and meet me. I hear you were promoted to Vice President of Procurement." Annie was greeting Andy Coach, a former co-worker at Titian.

"Yeah. Same position my father once held." Andy was happy to see her again.

"Bet you're doing well. High seven-figure salary, I'm sure," Annie inquired.

"Plus bonuses. And lots of perks," Andy bragged.

"Let's celebrate tonight. You aren't going anywhere, are you? I have plans for you…"

The next morning Annie woke up next to Andy with a huge smile on her face and an enormous feeling of satisfaction. She put one over on Peter. It was the same feeling she got when she landed a big contract with some sucker, or endlessly berated some loser, or sabotaged a rival. Most other people were insignificant, not worthy of notice. Her superiority was demonstrated yet again.

Later that month, Peter was saying, "Annie dear, I have such a good time with you. Why don't you divorce your husband? Then we can spend the rest of our time together, as long as this planet is still livable. I can handle the paperwork pro bono."

Annie's eyes widened again. "How soon can you start on it?"

*   *   *

Back at Thor's house, Vanessa had a gleam in her eye. "Darling, could we spend some time together today? You've been awfully busy lately. Wouldn't you like to balance it all out?"

Thor was looking through a stack of bills, fuming. "This is ridiculous! Food, utilities, everything we need just keeps going up and up. You would think in my position I would make more than enough to cover it. I'm probably the lowest paid director in the company. Conway just won't give me a raise or a promotion to vice president. He just throws me a bone with a token bonus every now and then."

"You know he's keeping you in your place. He thinks you are too ambitious. Why don't we see what else goes up and up? And I have a movie after that."

Thor was trying hard to calm himself. He loved his wife and there were definitely a few pleasures to be found at home. "How can I ever resist you?"

"Why would you ever want to?"

"No sane man could stand to be without you. Dinner first?"

"As long as it isn't one of your space meals."

"I have other delicacies in mind. Then maybe something to nibble on during the movie."

The next week, Thor's daughter Hannah was frantic, "Dad, he makes a lot of sense! Why would they send their planet just to kill everybody? They have to provide a way for us. They wouldn't just exterminate everybody for no reason."

Thor, trying to get her to think straight, replied, "Honey, there is no 'they.' Invader is a frozen planet where no life can survive."

Vanessa tried to reinforce the message. "Listen to your father!"

Hannah retorted, "It's a giant planet. Somewhere inside there has to be someone. I'm sure of it. It can't be any other way! Nothing else makes any sense."

Thor tried to reason with his daughter, "Listen, the galaxy is a gigantic shooting gallery with everything from asteroids and comets to rogue planets to neutron stars and black holes flying around everywhere. Catastrophes are statistical events that are sure to happen. This is one of them. That's all."

Hannah refused to listen. "No, Dad, everything has a reason. There is a purpose."

Chapter Thirteen
Failure

The Prime Minister was addressing the nation yet again:

"My friends, we live in the greatest and most powerful nation in the history of the world. This administration has noted there have been false reports that our special mission to Invader failed and there is some threat from that source. Your government is not convinced that such a failure occurred. In fact, the mission was partially successful. Everyone listening to me is urged to ignore those so-called experts and worry mongers being interviewed by the unauthorized, alternative press who are spreading this inflammatory view. They are ill-informed and it is a disservice to your country to pay attention to them.

"In order to reassure you that your government has succeeded and will ultimately prevail in its efforts to nullify this threat, I have authorized a third mission to finish the job of breaking up Invader and forcing it from its current path. Unfortunately, Capt. Flash Packard is no longer available to assist with future missions. Nevertheless, I am pleased to announce we will launch phase three of the mission tomorrow morning. Rest assured we will succeed in this effort…

"There is a movement in this country for people to empty their savings, quit their jobs, and just live it up, to indulge their fantasies. This by itself will lead to disaster. I am telling you that we must steer clear of this senseless ambition, where people want big houses and fashionable clothes and expensive cars and want it right now but don't want to work hard to accomplish those things. Everyone should endeavor to realize their full potential. That is what made our country great. This kind of errant behavior must be strongly discouraged…

"It has come to my attention that some of you have decided not to pay your taxes. Some of you think Invader will come and it won't matter. Let me be absolutely clear. Anyone avoiding the payment of their fair share will be fully prosecuted and incarcerated by the Justice Department. We have requested, and legislators have approved, the procurement of a new generation of tax robots to enforce payment. No bail will be permitted for suspected tax offenders…

"I know that many of you are dissatisfied with the pace of price increases. I know that for a few of you, your income might not have not risen to cover your expenses. I can promise you that your government is fully aware of the problem. As of today, price and profit controls are imposed by executive decree. All prices are hereby frozen. A committee has already been created to formulate specific policies. Your government is putting a stop to this situation. I have submitted legislation to create a new price control bureau. In addition, I am issuing an executive order requiring all employers to immediately grant all workers an across-the-board twenty per cent pay raise."

Off-camera, speaking to the vice chancellor, the prime minister asked, "How are we doing in our program to fortify and stock our bunkers? I'm counting on you to see to it and make sure it is done in complete secrecy."

The vice chancellor responded, "Mr. Prime Minister, everything is progressing according to plan."

Most people were now taking the threat from Invader seriously despite government and major media reassurances. Those who could afford to were dropping out of the work force, dropping out of schools en masse, spending down their savings, and borrowing whatever the banks and the government were willing to lend. However, credit was still becoming more and more difficult to obtain.

Widespread crime was a major public concern now. Prices of necessities and luxury goods were rising again while prices for other things dropped.

Some institutions, especially schools, went broke in increasing numbers.

As part of the new crime wave, hacking for fun and profit became a national sport. Hackers broke into computer systems to steal credit, to ship themselves goods they never paid for, to obtain government payments they never applied for, and to skim and embezzle funds anywhere they could.

Many saw no point in paying taxes, while many others saw their income dry up and couldn't pay their taxes anyway.

With revenues evaporating, the government was unable to pay its workers, its contractors, or welfare recipients and others dependent on public money. Only the military, policing agencies, legislators, and high-ranking officials were still getting paid, at least in part. This was the point in time when the government turned to massive money printing to cover their gaping deficits.

*　　*　　*

At Blaine Industries headquarters, Howard was instructing Brandon. "Price controls mean two things. Some things can no longer be produced at a profit. Nobody in their right mind is going to pay to produce something and give it away at a loss. That means shortages. We expected this to happen and planned for it. Now first, run all of the calculations again. Any product lines that can't be sold at a profit should be immediately shut down unless they are producing necessities we want to stockpile. In that case, the line should be shut down as soon as we have produced all we need for ourselves. Second, aggressively stockpile anything we have to buy from outside that will now be produced at a loss. Those items will soon disappear and become unobtainable."

"Right away. Highest priority. What about taxes? There are so many government agencies and policies that no longer serve any purpose with Invader on the way. Vacant buildings, pointless research, expensive unneeded defense procurements, spy agencies, paying farmers not to grow crops in the face of food shortages, maintaining unused equipment, education programs with no students, and environmental agencies are just a handful of examples. There are lots of other agencies that are useless, outdated, duplicated, or counterproductive to begin with, not to mention government credit cards and accounts that are predominantly misspent on personal items. Some institutes, boards that regulate geographic and other names, government PR agencies that advertise and try to sell government policies, captured regulatory agencies, and many more come to mind. Yet, I don't expect a single agency or program to be disbanded, because they all have their constituencies. There is enormous waste, and people can't afford it anymore. I don't think we should pay for it either. Any tax we can postpone should be delayed, even if they try to collect interest. Hold back any tax we think we can get away with not paying. At some point the government will lose control, and then any unpaid taxes will never be collected. Please get the accountants on it right away."

"You know, the dominant class will fight tooth and nail to maintain the status quo as long as they can. It's ironic that we ourselves are part of that privileged class."

*   *   *

Meanwhile at Titian, there was nothing to lose by preparing three laser/neutron beam weapons for launch. They were off-the-shelf orbiting weapon systems, launched by left over rockets of the type used for the old interplanetary probes. There was nothing new or risky and no problems were expected. They would launch in six months, well before the habitats were sent. Everything they needed was already in orbit.

*   *   *

Renee Jenner went to Thor's office. "Thor, I really want to spend some quality time with my sister before Invader strikes. We've all been working so hard our only time for family is when we can squeeze in a phone call once in a while. It's really important and I don't know how much longer there will be predictable transportation. Can you please give me a week off to go visit? I know some of the others feel the same way."

"I know the importance of family myself. You know the schedule's too tight for anyone to disappear for a week, and we have to worry about security, too. What if something happens and you can't get back?"

"Please? I have to!"

"I've already thought about this. I think the best thing to do is to bring families here to visit. We now have accommodations on the campus. If public or private transportation becomes a problem, I'll try to finagle a corporate jet and some fuel from our stockpile if it's absolutely necessary."

"Is it ok to kiss your boss?"

Renee Jenner didn't waste any time arranging for a visit from her older sister and only close relative. Some of the other astronauts made their own arrangements as well.

Before she left, Jenner's sister gave her a locket with pictures of her and her kids. Jenner promised the locket would always stay around her neck so she would never forget.

Norman Carson and his two brothers told stories to each other, like always, each trying to one-up the other. All three were successful professionals in their field. Norman asked them, "What will you do when it all freezes?"

Jerry Carson, a building inspector, answered first, "You know I have a lot of wealthy clients who are remodeling and stocking underground bunkers. I've been really successful navigating the bureaucracy, getting them their permits, expediting hearings, moving things along for them. I'm hoping one of them will allow me to live in their cave."

"I don't think there will be much use for building inspectors underground."

"Yeah, they need me now but when they are through with me, it's sayonara. I'm working on a new specialty they can use after Invader. I'm learning about agriculture and aquaculture. Triple threat. How can you turn that down? I'll be better at it than you are. One of them will have to keep me on."

"We'll see. What about you Harry?"

Harry Carson was an agent. His clients included some of the biggest names in sports and entertainment. "I know a lot of influential people. Some of them owe me big time. I plan to call in a few favors. They can get me into a cave with them. You know, I bet some of them will be invited into a cave just because of their celebrity status."

"Fair weather friends one and all I'll bet. You need a backup plan. As an agent, the best you can expect is to be invited to live in a cave ten per cent of the time."

"Very funny. You know how famous and important my clients are. It's a sure thing I'll get in somewhere."

*　　*　　*

Elsewhere at Titian, Conway was again on the phone in his office.

Barrow, Chairman of the Board, was complaining. "Conway, those big profits from the Invader intercept missions have just about dried up. Inflation makes them worth a lot less. On top of that the government is way behind in its payments to the company. Meanwhile, everyone on the board is complaining. This isn't some charity organization. Instead of pursuing your space mission, why don't you disband it and give us some extra dividends? We all need the money. Nobody escapes this kind of inflation."

Barrow didn't call the shots. Conway was irritated. "Why are you complaining? Your other companies made a pretty penny on the scam. Besides, I have us covered."

"How is that?"

"I used some of the profits to stockpile generous amounts of food, clothing, drugs, and other necessities. We rented a long-term preservation unit from Blaine for the perishables. As far as the stockholders are concerned, we're storing supplies we need for other contracts, including contracts related to the space mission. In actuality, all of the stuff is for you and the other board members and their families. By the time anyone figures it out, it will be too late to do anything about it. There should be enough to last you as long as you need. We're using the mission as a cover, so I'm not about to scrap it. Can you go along with that?"

Barrow thought about it for a few seconds. "Well, that might be Okay. I'm willing to wait and see. What about you?"

"I'm going into space. I'll be running the new colonies."

"I see."

"It's settled then. Time for me to get back to business."

* * *

At the Hurlock's house, in the Canaille settlement, Jenna was despondent. "Bad news, I was let go today. My class was getting too small. And, my last two paychecks bounced. And prices keep going up every single day. I'm trying to find tutoring jobs."

Chipper sighed and looked worried. "Yeah, we're barely making ends meet now. At least we used to have enough extra to store emergency food. Looks like we'll be spending even more time in the garden. Did you apply for unemployment benefits yet?"

"Yeah. I hope the government still has the money to pay me something and those checks don't bounce, too."

"Love you. We will manage one way or another. We still have each other." Chipper gave her a kiss.

Jenna had a thought that worried her even more. "How is your job? Will you still have work?"

Chipper reassured her. "There is still lots to do. Hughes is still paying me good money even though he still won't let all of us into his cave. Strange, nobody has seen him face-to-face for years, but everything still proceeds like normal. Don't worry."

* * *

Meanwhile, in another city, Zerathud hadn't received a single government pension payment for months. He hadn't been able to pay his real estate taxes and now the government, the same government that wasn't paying him, was threatening to take away his house because he wasn't paying them the money they weren't paying him!

Clearly, it was time for a drink. Zerathud went to the bar to meet Jimmy and his other buddies. There were maybe twenty-five or thirty people in the place.

"Hey Jimmy, you buyin'?"

Someone yelled out, "Nobody's buyin', we're all cut off. Have to pay your tab if you want a drink!"

Another voice shouted, "I ain't puttin' up with that crap! Haven't had no drink in two days and ain't about to get sober now!"

Next thing Zerathud knew, someone jumped over the bar and grabbed a liquor bottle. The owner fled into the street. Everyone helped themselves. Zerathud was already feeling high now though he'd only had a little bit of scotch. This was fun. They all spilled out onto the sidewalk and headed for a liquor store on the other side.

Zerathud felt great excitement as they all moved as one organism. They rushed the store, grabbing bottles off the shelves indiscriminately, helping themselves to the contents, chugging down the spirits as fast as they could manage. Fueled by alcohol, they started grabbing any bystander they could and demanding money.

Zerathud never thought he would be part of a mob. Now that he was, he didn't think at all. In fact, he was no longer consciously aware of anything, not even his buddy Jimmy next to him. He was part of the universal mind now.

There were sirens, way too loud, head splitting it seemed. They all started throwing bottles at the on-rushing policemen before he blacked out.

The newscasters dubbed it the liquor riots. They all passed out. After a while, they all started to wake up in the pokey. Zerathud remembered only the hazy outlines of what had happened and felt the gash on his head.

*   *   *

Maynard Kolar was livid. He couldn't sit still, couldn't eat, and couldn't concentrate on anything. He was completely consumed with hatred and jealousy. He had to do something.

Not only was Annie a public television celebrity, she also started a "Get Yours Now" club that included a buying service, and that people paid to join. But, that's not what was bothering him.

Now he knew, the tabloid rumors of Annie and her affair with the internet lawyer were all true, absolutely accurate. He realized yet again what a sucker he was and how she played him for a fool. He suffered at her hands all those many years, and for what? Annie and her boyfriend had to pay, plain and simple, and the sooner the better. He would make sure they suffered, like they were making him suffer. They didn't care about anyone else, so he wouldn't care either.

Maynard fumed. Annie was always obsessed with revenge, with getting even for every real or, more often, imagined slight. Now he decided it was his turn. He would get even and he wouldn't wait. Maynard's hatred for both of them irretrievably grew and he was consumed by it. More and more, it started to totally possess him. After all, what more could anyone do to him, anyway? So what if the authorities locked him away for life? That's only a few years, well worth it. As if anyone would bother to catch him anyway. They had more pressing issues to deal with, like being flung out into space and frozen and starved to death.

There was no real penalty for crime anymore. Maynard decided to steal a gun, right now. He would lay in wait somewhere for the two of them. They would suffer first before they died.

And where could he go to wait? Would they be at a hotel? At the big shot lawyer's mansion with its security? Did Annie have any new TV appearances anywhere? That would be easy to find out. He could search and call all of the networks, check upcoming schedules for all of the talk shows. He would wait outside the studio when she left. The only wrinkle was, he wanted to catch both of them together. It might take him several tries, but sooner or later, the lawyer would meet her or go with her. He could find a place to watch at a safe distance. Maynard's plan was sure to work.

Two weeks later, outside FiberVision Studios, Maynard saw the lawyer at the stage door in his limo, probably there to pick her up. Maynard covered himself up under one of the ubiquitous piles of garbage as he moved to get a clear line of fire. She emerged and started to duck into the limo. Maynard got off two shots with his laser rifle. He had an immense flush of satisfaction as he watched the lawyer crumple in a flash of heat. But what happened to Annie? He didn't know if he got her. Did she survive in the limo as it sped away?

Well, at least her sugar daddy was gone. Hope they weren't secretly married and she got a big inheritance. Maynard's divorce was not yet final, but nobody would care if it was bigamy these days. Wait, they couldn't be.

Time to make his getaway. He adjusted his knapsack full of food, worried about his pockets full of cashier's checks and his fully charged laser hand gun. Maynard had no detailed escape plan, only a simple econometric model: He would look for one of the ever more frequent mobs and join in, do whatever they were doing, find safety in numbers, and get lost in the crowd. He would listen to his police scanner to try and guess where the closest mob would be. Being an economist, Maynard's econometric model would perfectly predict what he should do, how he would hide, how the police would act, what Annie would do, and how he would escape. There was no question reality must conform to his model.

With the guidance of his model, Maynard could certainly evade the authorities for a long time. Long enough to get to Annie again if she had survived. Annie would be on her guard now, always looking over her shoulder. She would be forced to hire security, maybe a body guard. Let her worry. Let her worry herself sick.

Maynard could take his time. He thought to himself, there is no downside to crime anymore. We're all banksters now.

*   *   *

At a private compound on the West Coast, David James, self-proclaimed prophet, was preaching to his followers:

"I have heard from the inhabitants of Invader, indeed from the Supreme Being who rules this new, more perfect habitat. Their spirits descend upon me with their vital message.

"They are coming to gather the souls and spirits of a select few, those people who receive enlightenment and prove worthy to continue in a new and higher form of spiritual light.

"There will be a coming ordeal by fire and ice. Those true believers who come through the ordeal with their spirit intact, who show that they have earned a higher place in the cosmos, will be transported to Invader, to their new home. Invader is the stepping stone to the next plane of existence, a new plane more exalted than the lowly life we have experienced so far.

"This is the true meaning of the universe, stepping stones ascended one-by-one until we can finally reach perfection. Invader is the next stepping stone, but not the last. We must, each one of us, earn the right to advance to each next step, for every step on our journey to a perfected life.

"The planet Invader is inhabited by the Holy Ones who guided it here, the superior beings living the life of the next step, those who inhabit the planet. Why else would it come from the vast emptiness of space?

"The enlightened ones will survive together in eternal harmony and bliss, guided by the Holy Ones of Invader.

"There is a purpose. It is up to us to listen. We will wait patiently for them to come to us, then we will offer ourselves up to the higher cause. Those who don't listen will be cast out in agony."

*   *   *

Vanessa was at her house, reading a note from her daughter.

It said, "Dear Mom and Dad. I have gone to be with the initiates into the new life. Please do not worry about me. I will be fine. There is a place for us. We won't die with the planet. Be happy for me. Love, Hannah."

Vanessa was worried sick. "My god, Hannah ran off with that nut job David James and left a note! We have to do something!"

Thor, furious, declared, "Dammit, no telling what that fruitcake will do. Help me contact every authority and news source we can think of. Someone must know where they are. I will drag her back here if I have to."

Chapter Fourteen
Panic

The Prime Minister was addressing the nation:

"Your government has determined that our mission to Invader was not an unqualified success. Invader may, in fact, pose some slight level of threat at a point in our future. Your government is launching one final mission to finish what we started and divert and destroy this potential threat…

"Some of you are hoarding food, clothing, fuel, and other important items while your fellow citizens do without. Your government will not tolerate such selfishness. I have now issued an executive decree. Henceforth, anyone caught hoarding, with goods exceeding their immediate needs, will forfeit all of their possessions to the government and spend ten years in prison.

"There has been an increase in crime in some locations by groups with malicious intent. I have therefore submitted to the legislators a series of Vagrancy Acts. All public assemblies will henceforth require advance notification to the police and a permit from local authorities. This will be strictly enforced. I'm sure you will all understand the need for these measures.

"I am well aware that many of you think Invader will come and there is no reason to pay your taxes. We will not accept this irresponsible behavior under any circumstances. Anyone who refuses to do their fair share will be immediately jailed and then fully and vigorously prosecuted without recourse. Imprisonment will be swift and certain. There will be no exceptions.

"It has further come to my attention that many of you, individuals, merchants, and businesses alike, are refusing to accept this country's legal tender.

"I am aware that many merchants and individuals are demanding payment in goods instead of legal currency. This is a clear violation of the law of the land. This flagrant transgression is absolutely unacceptable and could lead to a breakdown in this great nation's financial system. Barter and swap arrangements constitute a threat to the well-being of every citizen and are hereby outlawed. I have issued an executive decree that any person who engages in any barter or swap transaction of any kind will be subject to immediate arrest and imprisonment for a minimum term of ten years. The same penalty will apply to anyone refusing to accept this country's legal tender in payment, whether electronic or printed.

"Now I know there have been complaints by Federal employees, contractors, and benefit recipients about not getting paid. This is a direct consequence of the refusal of miscreants to pay their legally mandated taxes, and is one of the reasons I am today imposing even harsher penalties and mandating the immediate arrest of tax evaders.

"I can assure all of you who are expecting government money that you will be paid in full. I have directed the central bank to provide all of the money necessary to meet the government's obligations."

People everywhere now realized the government could not save them and felt betrayed. Wholesale money printing and government lending, combined with faltering production, overwhelmed the scarcity of credit, resulting in hyperinflation. The hyperinflation was intensified since people had no use for money; rather, they craved food and necessities.

Police, military, government contractors and workers, and welfare recipients were now being paid again, but they were receiving increasingly worthless electronic currency that nobody wanted, and that didn't afford them much food.

Suicides and overdoses became so common the media rarely commented on it except in the case of celebrities.

Even ordinary people turned to crime and looting to try to quench their hunger and to make ends meet, joined by rogue police and bureaucrats. Police and military robots and drones were no longer well-maintained, so that enforcing order became increasingly problematic. Riots and flash mobs became commonplace. Government buildings were regularly set on fire, while many surviving, hidden government stockpiles were discovered and raided.

Panic was setting in.

*   *   *

Vanessa drove to a strip mall half a mile away to look for some vegetables to eat; fresh, frozen, or canned, it didn't matter. She would settle for anything she could find. There were no neighbors to go with her for safety on this trip; she had to go alone. She avoided the bus for fear of purse snatchings. If her car was stolen, well, she had a locator on it for all the good it would do, as long as she herself wasn't harmed. It was more likely that someone would steal the fuel cell from her car than the car itself. Nor did Vanessa care to go to a large overcrowded mall with only a handful of ineffective security robots.

She parked as close to the store entrance as she could. More than half of the stores in the strip were closed.

Most people's first instinct was to go to a large grocery store or to a farmer's market if they could find one, although farmer's markets were now becoming extinct. Vanessa discovered it was better to go to a health food store. People avoided these stores thinking the prices were way higher. They weren't, and the stores could no longer get health food to sell. They sold whatever they could find, a pot luck selection.

Prices were more than thirty-five percent higher than when she was there a week ago, and the shelves were three-quarters empty. She had to settle for asparagus, water chestnuts, beans, pears, peaches, and mushrooms, all canned. Credit cards were no longer accepted anywhere, and she hadn't brought enough cash to afford the new higher prices. She needed more money from the ATM at the store, but when she tried to get it, withdrawals were blocked. She took as much of the canned fruits and vegetable as she could afford and left. As she was leaving, a flash mob broke into the convenience store at the end of the strip. It was time to speed out of there as fast as she could.

*   *   *

The world went from high inflation to hyperinflation in less than three months. People began to pay attention when the government promised unlimited amounts of electronic money to pay its creditors; to bail out the banks; to provide food, rent and other assistance; and to guarantee all deposits and many delinquent loans people and corporations refused to pay. People were already withdrawing their money from surviving banks and, for the few lucky ones, to live it up while they still could. With the implicit admission that the banks needed to be rescued, this now turned into a torrent of instant electronic withdrawals. That made the banks even less solvent and turned into an accelerating vicious circle, requiring a dizzying binary blizzard of newly created cash nobody wanted.

Government spokesmen appeared regularly to assure people that their money was both safe and useful, it was all one hundred percent guaranteed, they would back it while keeping a lid on inflation with their price controls, there was no need for panic and withdrawals, and no need for the illegal practice of barter. It was a joke, and nearly everyone knew it. By the time the government finally declared a bank holiday and froze all accounts it was too late. The electronic cat was long since out of the digital bag. It had all escalated at the speed of light.

Things progressed to the point that prices were changing 2, 3, and 4 times a day while cash wages changed only monthly. When people finally received their paychecks, the money wouldn't buy much of anything if it was even accepted anywhere. They were working for next to nothing, so why bother? Except that there weren't a lot of necessities left to buy or steal, either.

Shops had the same problem. Much of their expenses and purchases had to be paid for immediately, but many receivables took a long time to arrive, if they ever did. Debtors were in no hurry to pay up. As a result, a great many shops just simply closed, leading to more scarcities. Business and individuals delayed payment of bills and taxes, trying to pay in money that was worth less all the time. Some retailers kept goods off the shelf waiting for higher sales prices, leading to mostly empty stores.

The economy was starting to collapse. Riots and looting became ubiquitous.

The remaining police focused on keeping the mobs from laying their hands on the politicians, leaving the troublemakers and ordinary people to themselves.

Many people lost all of their savings. Even for those who found a way to hang onto their money, it did them little good.

Those who had gardens, if they could protect them, fared the best.

*   *   *

At Blaine Industries headquarters, Howard was obsessing on security. He was worried about his hidden stockpiles being discovered, Blaine Industries being labeled a 'hoarder,' and consequently seeing his supplies confiscated by the government, in which case they would be distributed to the political classes and their benefactors.

Most stockpiles were hidden in secret underground tunnels, to be moved to the main cave before it was sealed off. By then it would also be time to distribute the surplus necessities they couldn't use or barter to worthy organizations like the Reverend Franklin.

A few people got rich taking out large loans before the inflation and buying goods with the money while they still could. The Blaines were among them. Some people took out big loans but squandered the money. Now they were broke, and couldn't even pay the ever-depreciating interest.

Blaine industries still had something of a cash flow. They decided they may as well pay off their loans for the record, with cheap money.

*   *   *

Once he was back home, Forbes rushed to see his former girlfriend. "I couldn't wait to see you again. I'm so happy you want to be together and start over. I have some tickets for tonight."

Page 151

"I'm sorry but I already have plans."

"I thought you said you were waiting to go out and get reacquainted again. A lot has happened since the last time we were together. Let's go somewhere tonight and catch up."

"I already have a date. You didn't think you were the only one, did you?" she asked.

"Well, yes. I thought we were going to resume our relationship where it left off."

"I'm sorry. Have you heard Annie Kolar? With things as they are, I couldn't possibly commit to just one man. It's a time to have all the enjoyment you can before it's too late. There's no point to exclusive relationships anymore. You can see for yourself there's no future in that."

"I'm acquainted with Ms. Kolar." Forbes suddenly realized how fickle his supposed girlfriend was. She had moved on, lost interest, and was only playing with him all along. Well, that certainly was a short rekindled relationship. "I'll be going now."

Forbes was staying in his modest childhood home. The neighborhood was no safer than any other these days, but he had taken precautions.

For one, he set up an indoor garden in the attic. Whenever he returned home, he attended to it. He had already installed skylights between a pair of solar panels several years before to supplement the unpredictable electric lighting. Both he and his mother hoped nobody would suspect or detect the garden and it could continue to produce year-round.

For another thing, he had refurbished a fuel cell Titian was discarding, and he hooked it up to some resistance heaters to keep warm when the utilities failed. All of his improvements and emergency supplies were set up secretly and without permits or any other public record.

Upon his return home, Forbes's mother was crying. "What's wrong?" he asked.

"I have some terrible news. Your sister, her husband, and a friend went into the city to see if they could find some food and trade their car or some clothes for it, but they got caught in a flash mob. Her friend called me while you were out. She and her husband were killed in the riot. Nobody knows who shot her, it was too chaotic, and nobody bothers to investigate anything anymore. We only have each other now.

"John, I would like to know that someone from this family survived. Please don't worry about me. After you've stayed with me a while longer, I want you to go back to the space program. You have a chance to outlast this madness and do something important. Just promise you will visit me whenever you can before the expedition leaves."

"There are astronaut apartments at Titian. If they will accept me back in the program, why don't you move there so I can look after you? You'll be safer there anyway."

"I would like that."

Forbes knew Thor would take him back if he was enthusiastic enough, as long as he caught up with the project plans, problems, and developments. As an exogeologist, his expertise overlapped with other astronauts' specialties such as climate and agriculture. He could help to identify mineral resources, water, types of soils, rates of erosion, and similar features on the new planet. Now he must try to re-dedicate himself, find some genuine motivation somehow, and overcome his natural skepticism.

Once back at Titian, Forbes sought out his most recent flame Renee Jenner. If they were going to work together on this mission, they needed to patch things up. "Do you think we can be friends again?" he asked her.

"So, you've decided you want to be a space pig after all. Neither of us has much family. I'm leaving behind a sister and you're leaving your mother. Anyway, I'm sorry to tell you our relationship will be strictly professional from here on. After you left, I decided to dedicate myself entirely to the program. I want to concentrate on the mission and spend whatever spare time I have with my sister. I really don't have time for you outside the project."

*　　*　　*

Conway was relaxing at his tropical private resort island when the phone interrupted him.

"This had better be important, Barrow."

(Pause) "I'm well aware the defense committee is investigating us for profiteering on our Invader contracts. I have contacts on all the legislators' staffs who keep me informed. What's your point?"

(Pause) "They're just grandstanding for the public. There's nothing to worry about. You know most legislators put their assets in a blind trust. It's just a fig leaf. Everyone on the committee owns Titian stock in their trust. We offered them cheap stock options to make sure. All we have to do is accidentally relax our security, and the bots that crawl the web and write the news will discover they have a conflict of interest and tell everyone about it. Besides, we employ key relatives of a lot of legislators at inflated salaries and they know it."

(Pause) "My strategy? We remind them of what they have to lose by public exposure. At the same time, we give them something innocuous to parade in front of the voters when they are trolling for votes. I plan to give them some nonsense about inadequate accounting controls."

(Pause) "Don't worry. I've had plenty of experience handling those morons. Why don't you call my secretary and arrange for the key politicians to fly to my island on a 'fact-finding' pleasure junket?"

(Pause) "Fine. Don't disturb me again. I'll call *you*."

*　　*　　*

Time and resources for the project were running out.

Some of the prospective astronauts expressed reservations about their survival chances and the many unknowns of this mission. Some worried about whether the remaining tight schedule could be achieved. A few of them had already dropped out. Enough of them still remained to launch the mission, but Thor realized whether to stay was a personal decision each of them had to make.

Government payments to Titian nearly dried up, that is, they were being paid in increasingly worthless electronic currency. The company was no longer able to issue bonds. Many production lines had to be shut down due to lack of workers or lack of materials, despite production being mostly robotic. This was true for some of Titian's subcontractors as well. Titian anticipated this situation from the beginning, but how good was their panning? Had they stockpiled enough materials and spares, and did they send everything they could to their geostationary facilities? Were their ground-based assets well enough protected? Did they store away enough extra food and necessities for their employees, enough to keep key people on the job?

Several of the staff asked Thor, "What about these oaths you passed out for us to sign? What is this all about?"

"Conway is demanding that all of us, me included, sign his contract saying that when the mission reaches the new planet all of us will report to him, that he will be the absolute and permanent world-wide Prime Minister and Commander, and that you will obey all of his orders immediately without question. Please just sign it. I can't say publicly what else you can do with it.

"Just think for yourselves. When you arrive at the new planet you will encounter problems we can't predict. You will need to use your expertise and experience, and to work together to analyze and formulate a plan of action. Even so, you will make mistakes. What kind of organization will you need?

"Think, how far into interstellar space do the laws of this planet extend? Where in outer space is the authority to enforce contracts made on this planet? That's everything I can safely say on the subject."

Thor was also asked, "Will Conway join us for the rest of our training?"

The answer: "No, he is much too busy to train with you. We've arranged for customized one-on-one training for him a month before launch."

*　　*　　*

Around the same time, at the Hurlock's house, Jenna was panicking.

"Someone stole all of our fish and vegetables from the garden! And our canned food is almost gone!"

"Then we'll have to make do with what we preserved in the attic. Where are the kids? It isn't safe out there anymore." Chipper was getting to the end of his rope.

Just then, Leah and Ted were coming down the stairs. Ted was agitated. "Dad, there's a lot of noise outside."

First there was a swishing sound, then a crescendo of loud noises and voices. Sirens started blaring. There was a loud hiss coming from somewhere down the street.

Jenna looked out the window, horrified. An acrid burning odor filled the air. Some houses were on fire. People were running around everywhere. "There's a large crowd about four blocks from here and they're headed this way," she worried.

"Daddy, I'm scared." Leah was turning white.

"Be brave. It's time to find the Reverend. We will spend the rest of our time with him, all of us together when we make it out of here. You know we took his advice and made an escape plan."

All four of them headed for the back door at once.

Only a week before, Chipper bought a laser rifle and pistol on the street. It was a felony to own these weapons, and some people who bought them on the street got caught, but he felt there was no choice. Plenty of laser weapons were homemade. They were easy to put together with industrial parts. However, Chipper didn't care to experiment with something that could prove vital to his family's survival.

He already stuffed the trunk of his car with freeze dried food, water, warm clothes, a tent, torches, air mattresses, and other emergency supplies. He kept his car's fuel cell fully charged now and parked it on a parallel back street. He grabbed his laser rifle, pistol, and a ladder.

He also figured the best route would be to take back roads to a major highway and stick with it. Automatic traffic monitors would detour him around road blocks and hazards. He would drive on manual control on the secondary roads, but could not override automatic navigation on the highways.

"Hurry, hurry!" he commanded as they ran to the back door. The mob was advancing down his street. As they ran out, they heard loud shouts and a crash. Someone was breaking in the front door, probably to loot the place! "Run as fast as you can!"

They ran for the wooden stockade fence in the back. Chipper put the ladder up and helped Jenna over, then started to lift up the children and hand them to her on the other side, all to the accompaniment of shouts and noise coming from his house. As he was handing Ted over to Jenna, his back door burst open. Someone yelled, "Look, there they are! Get them."

As Chipper furiously climbed and balanced at the top, starting to yank the ladder over with him, he heard two whoosh sounds from a laser rifle. Two spots at the top of the wooden fence popped and burst into flames.

Chipper fell to the other side, heart pounding. "Run! Run! They're coming for us!"

They got to the next fence and scrambled over, full of adrenaline. As Chipper plunged to the ground, he glimpsed his fence in the distance falling down, being forced over by their pursuers. "They're right behind us!"

They headed for their car. Jenna got there first and thumbed the doors open. They all jumped in while she reached over from the passenger side and started the electric motor. As soon as Chipper was in the driver's seat they raced away, just as the second fence was falling.

By now Leah was shrieking hysterically. "Mommy! Mommy! One of those men looks like Cathcart. I'm scared. He might get me!"

"It's okay, Leah. Cathcart died a long time ago. Those were desperate starving people. They can't hurt us now. We will see Reverend Franklin soon. Daddy will get us there safely. Don't worry."

Once they got to the highway, the trip would be out of their hands unless the computers that controlled the highways failed. That wasn't out of the question with vandalism and mobs breaking into government buildings right and left.

As the Hurlocks drove away, Chipper could see four or five people spilling out onto the street and doing something with a parked car. "Hang on!" he told everyone as he hit the accelerator. "Once a mob gets an idea in its head it obsesses on it. I think they are going to try to steal a car and maybe catch us."

Jenna said, "Oh! You almost missed the corner! I'll watch the navigation and let you know where to get around the backups. I think rioters will try to be where there's congestion and easy targets. We should avoid places like that, and avoid where there might be looting."

Everyone was hanging on as the car sped and squealed around corners, blasted right past stop signs and through red traffic lights.

"Really, if we ever go home again you will have a mailbox full of computer-generated government love notes. You'll get so many tickets they'll never let you drive again!"

"And no matter how crazy I drive, there's a car following us. We have to get to the highway so the computers will keep it away from us."

"You'll make it. Just don't let up now!"

Reverend Franklin had selected a mountainous area for his retreat. Highways led to the valley from two different directions, and it was possible to detour and get from one road to the other if the there was a blockage. Two different two-lane roads led up to the retreat from the base and there was no other easy access to it. Security robots protected the roads while other cameras and robots scanned for climbers.

The compound itself was a hastily built ramshackle affair, almost a shanty town.

"We'll be there in an hour or two. It won't be luxurious but there will be food and water and maybe heat for the cold nights," Clifford tried to reassure everyone. Yet, he himself wasn't so sure. Was he doing the right thing leading his family to the reverend? Should he have let himself feel so compelled to follow? Maybe he should have pressed Hughes harder to let all four of them into his cave. He hoped he had chosen the best path.

All of them hoped there would be no more disturbances once they arrived at the valley.

*　　*　　*

Meanwhile, at Titian headquarters, Michael burst into Thor's office.

"Sorry to barge in on you, but a mob broke through security and destroyed the space elevator. Only the offshore elevators remain."

"Holy crap! Do we still have our emergency backup shuttle capability and boosters?"

"Yeah, they haven't gotten to our shuttle hangars yet."

"Get all of the security to the shuttle launch area as fast as you can.

"The astronauts are still in training, but I'm worried something might happen to the shuttles. Better keep them fueled and ready to go. If a mob gets anywhere near the launch area, we'd better send the astronauts and their cryogenic units up right away. I still want to wait as long as possible to send them into space because the reduced gravity atrophies muscles and bones. Get them to our new planet in the best shape possible. But if we have to go sooner, so be it."

*　　*　　*

A few days later, somewhere to the West, David James was addressing his followers at their compound.

"The time has come to progress to the next step in our spiritual journey. The spirit of Invader has come upon me. They are ready to gather the worthy. All is prepared. There is no longer anything to prevent the ordained destiny of this planet. Our future now lies elsewhere. The people of this planet have betrayed themselves, betrayed us, and now this planet is doomed. The die is cast, the game is over. Our time has come, our troubles will be lifted away and we will be vindicated..."

Sometime later, a computerized news report stated, "The bodies of one thousand two hundred and forty-seven cult members were found yesterday, apparently suicides. It appears they all succumbed to self-inflicted poisoning. They apparently died willingly, with blissful smiles on their faces. They were followers of David James, who was also among the dead. We will have additional details as they become available."

Thor and Vanessa were both suddenly overwhelmed, their minds and bodies completely limp. What they feared most had come to pass.

"This is my fault," Thor said darkly. "You were right. I should have been here. I shouldn't have spent so much time at the office."

"Please don't think that way," Vanessa said, trying to soothe him.

Six days later, Thor and Vanessa had been sleep walking the past five days and still were, right through the funeral. Although they made the necessary arrangements, it was as if someone else was doing it. The words they and others uttered at the ceremony came from some distant, nearly inaudible place, they couldn't tell where. The words just drifted by, never really understood.

The next day Thor's secretary was waiting for him when he finally returned. "Thor, Conway wants to see you in his office at once."

When Thor arrived, Conway spoke. "I see things are coming to a head. When you have everything under control and the success of this mission is assured, I want Michael to take over. As soon as that time comes this company will no longer need your services. Give me weekly reports until then and get everything in order as quickly as possible. You have one month to make the transition and resolve whatever issues you have to. Now go back to your office."

<h1 style="text-align:center">Chapter Fifteen</h1>
<h2 style="text-align:center">Getting Even</h2>

The Prime Minister was again addressing the nation:

"Your government has determined that Titian Space Systems and its CEO misled this government and this nation regarding the magnitude of the effort required to divert Invader. While we have determined that Invader no longer poses a threat, in the interest of prudence your government has today launched a fourth and final mission to the planet in order to provide absolute assurance of that fact…

"There has been entirely too much skepticism and naysaying, and sensationalism concerning the non-threat posed by Invader. I have therefore directed your government to press forward with its investigation of all news organizations, sources, blogs, and other public outlets who are purveyors of false information. Spreading of unfounded rumors is detrimental to public confidence and safety, and is an act of treason and a form of sabotage, and will henceforth be prosecuted as a capital offense…"

*　　*　　*

Shortly thereafter, Conway answered his phone, "Yes Picador, what is it?"

"You know what an extremely vindictive man the Prime Minister is, and you made a public fool of him. He just introduced emergency legislation into my committee to immediately cancel all Titian projects and halt all payments to your company. That will play with the voters and legislators who are questioning why we still need big space and defense contracts anyway. He wants an immediate vote in committee and then on the floor. The legislation will be closed to debate and amendments. I thought I should be the first to tell you."

"You're the chairman. I expect you to table it. You well know I can destroy your career if I want to. I'm pretty vindictive myself, you know."

"My hands are tied. It's an emergency measure. Besides, I have a choice between your stick and a Prime Minister's carrot. I would certainly prefer the carrot as the lesser of the evils. I'm sorry, but I have to return to the committee now."

"Dammit, Picador, I told you to table it or there will be consequences."

"This can't happen. It's time to pull out all the stops," Conway muttered to himself. He buzzed his secretary.

"Judy, get me Picador's daughter-in-law. I want to fire her personally. Then tell our public relations VP to call a press conference."

Later at the press conference, Conway made his statement. "Ladies and gentlemen of the press, the Prime Minister has leveled some serious charges against Titian Space Systems. In the interest of fairness to the public and our shareholders, I would like to set the record straight. A number of years ago, the Prime Minister contacted me personally about Invader and asked about the seriousness of the threat. I explained to him that Invader was a gas giant and that there was no possibility of diverting it from its course. The Prime Minister insisted on proceeding anyway against my best advice. As a patriot, I had no other choice than to obey. Rest assured, Titian will not accept the role of scapegoat for this transparent and misguided, politically motivated policy…"

Later that day, Conway's secretary interrupted him, "Barrow is on the phone and he says it's urgent."

"Put him through.

"What is it this time, Barrow?"

"Haven't you heard? The government is preparing to audit Blaine Industries' warehousing division. They heard about Titian's stockpiles of food, clothing, and other goods that were stored for us. They are accusing you personally of hoarding and intend to swear out a warrant for your immediate arrest based on their accusations. You will be locked up without bail same as any other accused hoarder. This is coming straight from my contacts in the Prime Minister's palace, so there is nobody you can bribe. You promised all of us board members that we and our families would have food and necessities, so now what? You better find a way to make good. I'm going to recommend to the board that they vote to dissolve the company, declare bankruptcy, sell off all the assets for whatever they can get, and distribute the proceeds. When the government pulls our funding today or tomorrow, the board feels it will have no choice except to terminate you as president and CEO of the company."

"If you follow through on your threats, make no mistake, I will ruin you and anyone on the board who votes with you."

Conway thought out his options. He could wait for the Prime Minister to obtain his warrant and for the government police robots to come to Titian to arrest him, or he could flee to another continent in his corporate jet and hide somewhere, or he could see if a shuttle was scheduled to take-off for the geosynchronous facility and bump whoever he had to and get on it, or he could take his helicopter to the marine space elevator complex and risk the radiation to get to orbit and the space complex.

The best bet was to find a shuttle that was ready for launch. The government could send some other company's shuttle to fetch him, but he would make sure they were denied docking privileges at Titian's geosynchronous facility. He would wait there until his habitat was launched. In the meantime, his whereabouts must remain secret as long as possible.

Conway left his office at once and told nobody where he was going.

*   *   *

Annie addressed her internet and television faithful, perhaps for the last time. "Cave projects are failing, space colonization is failing, and the only thing left is to go for life now, live it up as long as you can. That's the only option left. You will never have another chance. What do you need to enjoy yourself right now, this minute? When else will you get another chance? Never, so don't wait, don't hesitate.

There isn't a minute to lose. Nothing is stopping you. Go for it right now and let nothing stand in your way..."

Annie's confidence started to wane. A slight uncertainty crept into her voice. As far as she knew, Maynard could be lurking anywhere and her life could end at any moment. Instead of concentrating on having fun she was worrying more about food and necessities. People knew she had goods and food stashed somewhere. She might well be the target of a mugger or a stalker.

She was a public figure. There was no way to maintain a low profile. She had to look over her shoulder every minute. Her body guards quit to take care of themselves, and her robots weren't reliable without their handlers. She had no husband or fiancé to watch out for her anymore. Her boy toys had all turned away to more serious matters. It was taking a toll. She was starting to look older than her true age.

Annie's days were numbered now, and she was starting to struggle with cold hard reality. Her wants and her pursuits were losing their meaning as the harshness of her impending doom moved from the unreal depths of her mind to the front of her gaze.

Serious hesitation dominated her mind for the first time in her adult life.

*   *   *

Food was now the most important asset anyone could own, as long as nobody else knew about it. Anyone who was known to have food was certain to be robbed, whether by a lone thief or a gang.

People had long since stopped relying on big media for their news. News was written mainly by robots that crawled the web and regurgitated electronic blurbs and government releases, along with other self-serving press releases, with the results self-censored for political correctness. Most of the populace got their news from blogs, friends, infomercials, and tabloids, but then it was impossible to ferret out what was true and reliable from what wasn't. Consequently, rumor and innuendo ruled the day.

Grocers' shelves, farms with their fields and barns, and any food warehouses and government stockpiles that weren't well-protected were stripped bare. Bakers, grain dealers, convenience stores, nobody was spared. Anyone connected with the food industry was certain to have their homes broken into and ransacked. Desperate people would eat anything they could get their hands on. Any book or article by Euell Gibbons was at premium and had to be hidden away.

Rumors flew.

There were reports of hungry mobs venting their frustration on agricultural workers and bureaucrats, grocers, bulk dealers, and everyone else who might possibly know the location of unpublicized food supplies. Other reports stated bands of marauders boarded docked container and cruise ships allegedly loaded with food or grains, wrecking their engines so they couldn't escape while they were being looted.

Government price controls only exacerbated the shortages. There were stories about troops that were called out in attempts to restore order. According to the stories, instead of controlling the rioters, some troops joined in, and then the violence escalated. Officials tried to unmask alleged hoarders but few were found and prices soared stubbornly higher.

In one case in the news, local officials lectured the populace on conservation and the evil of hoarding food beyond one's immediate needs when they were shouted down and then attacked and beaten by rioters while on the air, with the rioters demanding food handouts.

In another case, when rioters attacked a public building rumored to have hidden food supplies, police shot and killed three of the rioters, which only caused the trouble to escalate. In the end, more than 200 rioters were injured or killed and many buildings were set on fire. Several officials committed suicide rather than fall into the hands of the mob.

The truth of these rumors was impossible to determine. Only one thing was certain. Most people wanted a scapegoat and were ready to blame, get even with, and wreak vengeance on whoever they didn't happen to like. All it took was a demagogue with a pointy finger to set off the tinderbox, and there was no shortage of sociopaths anxious to work the crowd and use the situation to their advantage.

*　*　*

Michael brought the news about Titian and Conway to Thor. "We still have workers to pay and some equipment left to buy. How can we do that with our funding reduced? Our secret stash may not be enough."

"What if the government decides to confiscate our mission supplies that aren't in-orbit and they try to shut us down?"

"Michael, I don't think we have to worry about that. It helps that some influential members of the public are in favor of this project, thanks to Rev. Franklin and our other publicity outlets. I don't think it would be politically expedient for the Prime Minister or the legislature to shut us down. We have bigger problems than that, anyway."

"You're referring to the minilabs?"

"The minilabs, the sets of custom hybrid seeds, the soil micronutrients and other agricultural supplies, the temporary shelters, and things like that. Blaine is making them, but we can't pay for them if our funding dries up.

"There's more. I didn't tell you before, but Conway fired me from Titian effective at the end of the month. You will have to take over the project."

"I can't do that. You are the only one who understands every aspect of this project. If you go, we're all in trouble."

*　*　*

Meanwhile at Blaine Industries, Howard was talking to Rube Goldstein.

"Howard, there won't be enough oxygen to support twelve thousand people. The agricultural crops won't produce enough of it, even though we're planning for a crop surplus and emergency food storage. We planned large underground lakes stocked with fish and phytoplankton that would produce the rest of the oxygen we need, but we can't make them large enough to give us any spare margin. As we mine the cave, there will be opportunities for expansion of the lakes, but not at first.

"The answer is surface mining of the frozen atmosphere, but we need more mining robots and can't make them ourselves. They have to be able to work at minus 390°F. We also need self-contained CO_2 recycling machinery that does require outside air that will keep us going the first year or two. We don't have enough of that either."

"How many can we support?"

"I figure seventy-five hundred."

"Looks like I owe Brandon and Tim an apology. They were right all along. It was still worth planning big. I will let everyone know."

Chapter Sixteen
Mob Rule

Now was the moment of truth, when stark reality intruded, when those in denial were forced to face the truth of what was happening.

The Prime Minister was once again addressing the country:

"Let me be absolutely clear. Unwarranted panic and pessimism are far too prevalent. Gangs, vigilante groups, and flash mobs are forming all too often. We will not allow law and order to break down. We are one people, all of us pledging allegiance to this great planet, all of us defending our country. Therefore, I am hereby declaring martial law. Army robots and drones are even now being deployed everywhere. Your government demands order, and we will achieve peace…"

Off camera, speaking to the vice chancellor, he said, "We have to maintain law and order long enough to safely reach our bunker. Is everything prepared?"

The vice chancellor responded, "We can be ready to depart in a day and a half."

Desperation was the order of the day. Law and order was non-existent and it was far too late to do much about it. Gangs marked out their territories and took whatever they wanted from hapless residents. Not even the homeless were spared. The gangs were countered by vigilante groups that sprang up like weeds. The vigilantes in turn felt fully justified exterminating anyone and everyone they suspected of being a gang member, or just plain didn't like. There was no time or need for trials or for fact-finding. The gangs responded in kind. Every block and borough had its own private wars with ever-shifting allegiances.

As always, food was the most precious commodity. The only way to get some, if any was to be found, was to steal it or barter for it. Nobody would accept currency or even gold. Everyone wanted usable goods, necessities.

Ordinary people, just trying to survive, tried to maintain a low profile and to hide whatever stockpiles of food and necessities they had, if they even had any in the first place.

Many of the wealthy and those with large businesses maintained private security robot forces, helicopters, bunkers and underground living spaces. This gave them a means to try to stay ahead of the mobs that spontaneously came and went. Those with bunkers realized that now was the time to seal themselves in for better or worse.

Most of the police and military had deserted by now, and the few who remained sided with the people; some joined gangs in an effort to obtain food. A few knew the locations of government bunkers and led gangs to try to break in. Others commandeered drones with ground-penetrating radar, using them to try to locate caves and underground dwellings. For those few police and military that were still loyal, their prime responsibility was to use robots, drones, and any other means still at their disposal to protect the politicians. Ordinary people were left to fend for themselves.

Jailers abandoned the prisons to take care of themselves, leaving the prisoners to feed on rats and foul water. It wasn't long after that before the large prison population found their escape. They poured out onto the streets to rejoin their old gangs to angrily prey on anyone and everyone.

*   *   *

A mob had gathered at a government grain elevator and warehouse in the middle of the country.

Maynard joined in and moved as one with the mob, shouting to the top of his lungs. He felt inspired, empowered. This was a time when people could take their lives back. It was a time to feel and act as one formidable being, as an autonomous, nameless, spontaneous animal. He not only felt his own excitement but the added excitement of the crowd. He felt a unity, an inviolable need to stay together. Everyone was shouting in a deafening cacophony. The crowd flowed like a single newly evolved organism with a unitary, though evolving, purpose.

A thin rank of police robots creaked in, spewing black smoke and tear gas as they were programmed to do. The mob held together despite choking, gasping, burning eyes. Someone commandeered a government truck, then another and another. They bore down on the robots. As the robots turned their attention to the trucks, firing their laser cannons. Meanwhile, others in the mob broke through the fences and smashed into the grain storage.

The few human guards dropped their laser rifles and fled for their lives. Some of them didn't made it.

The ever-escalating noise and violence culminated in a mad rush to the warehouse and grain elevator. Many were trampled, unnoticed.

The mob unloaded their venom on the now barely functional robots, unloading the newly acquired laser rifles, heavy rocks, and tree branches on the senseless behemoths, rendering them total scrap.

People stuffed their pockets, coats, bags, and anything that could serve as a container with food and grain before leaving. No reinforcements came to stop the looting.

It was a feeling of great power and satisfaction, of sweet victory. Some lay dead, cooked by lasers with a charred stench, but they just appeared like sleeping dogs in the grass, not worthy of attention.

Maynard had long since forgotten about Annie. He was intoxicated with this feeling of raw animal power, loaded with adrenaline. His old life had evaporated and not even a glimmer of a memory of it remained. The old Maynard no longer existed and would never return. Power and hatred possessed him completely. His transformation was complete.

*   *   *

Rev. Franklin gathered tens of thousands of his followers on the mountain top. Well, actually a tall hill. He had plenty of donated food, warm clothing, tents, and security robots. He ministered to the crowd while they waited for the divine will to manifest itself. "This is our final test. We shall face it with dignity, faith, perseverance, courage…"

*　　*　　*

Thor was more depressed than he ever thought possible. Michael was barely able to get his attention.

It was time for Michael to seize the initiative. He had become acquainted with Brandon Blaine and gave him a call.

"We need some agricultural material and survival gear if you have it. We don't have the cash flow to pay for it. Anything you can part with? I also want to get into the warehouses we leased from you but we can't pay the back rent. Maybe you need something of ours."

"As a matter of fact, we do need a few things."

"What will it cost us?"

"This is no time for accounting. You give us whatever you can scrounge up, especially robots, and we'll do the same for you," Brandon said. "Do you have any of the new MSF27 security robots?"

"Only three and they're guarding the offshore space elevator. It's impossible to get more. Shall we proceed?"

"Immediately. There's no time to waste. I'll arrange secure private shipment as soon as the inventory is ready and I expect you to do the same."

"Agreed. We have a deal."

Michael ran to Thor's office.

"Boss, I've been doing some freelancing. Blaine Industries needs surface mining equipment and CO_2 recyclers. We have mining units that can operate reliably on asteroids in near absolute zero temperatures. We also have prototype CO_2 to O_2 converters from the geosynchronous complex we won't need anymore. We can exchange our bots and recyclers for the minilabs, agricultural and survival gear they built for us. They will also allow us to get into their warehouses to try and retrieve some of the food Conway stored there for himself and

Page 171

the board before the government shows up to claim it. We can pay our own workers in food and clothing. By my reckoning, we can complete the mission and Blaine can finish his cave."

"I think it's too late now."

"What would your father have said?"

"You're right, let's go for it. Since Conway disappeared, nobody knows I'm being fired yet. The mission is the most important thing of all."

"Quite the rebel, aren't you?"

Thor picked up the phone and called Conway's secretary. "Judy, this is Thor. I heard a rumor that Conway is trying to escape to the geosynchronous facility. While he's on his way, I want you to route all his calls and communications concerning the colonization project to me with notification or copies to Michael. And get me through to Conway now. Despite what you say, I'm sure he left you instructions how to get hold of him if anything urgent came up."

A few minutes later, Thor was talking to Conway. "While you are incommunicado, I will be handling all project details from here with Michael's help. Michael and I have agreed that if I am fired, he will quit. He's the only other one who can see the project through to completion, so I'm afraid you're stuck with the both of us until the mission is launched."

"You don't run this company and you're both insubordinate. The two of you are fired immediately, right now."

"And who will carry out that order, and who else will finish this project? Remember, you are in hiding."

"Don't be so cocky. This will all blow over very soon. Then I get my revenge on you two. You and the Prime Minister will find out you have bigger fish to fry while I am here deciding *your* fate. The public has already turned its attention back to survival. The Prime Minister's only reason to pursue me now is personal revenge and his own political survival supersedes that."

"Guess what then? Everything has disintegrated. The old order and the old rules are already dissolving right before your eyes. The corporate structure is dead. You have no scope to operate anymore.

People will only live on in the caves and on the planets we conquer, so who will listen to you?"

"You are wrong. I am well aware of the situation. That's why people like me who realize it are so unpredictable and dangerous. Most people don't acknowledge any permanent change and never will. They will cling to the belief that this is just some aberration until it's too late. They will still dance to my tune in their willful ignorance, and I will still have the power to do what I want. You and Michael better be worrying. I won't tolerate your behavior. It's totally offensive and mark my words, you will pay for it."

"Like you say, I have bigger fish to fry right now. If there is the slightest misstep, we'll miss the launch schedule."

Thor ordered his staff on the in-orbit facility to deny Conway docking privileges. Now it was a matter of loyalties. And nobody there wanted Conway at the station or on the mission. Would they afraid to defy Conway's orders and let him?

*　　*　　*

At Blaine Industries headquarters, a mob was forming outside the main cave entrance. There was another mob outside the headquarters offices ready to break in. How would they get to the cave now?

Howard's secretary joined him in his office. "There is a Ms. Annie Kolar here who insists on seeing you. She says she used to work for Titian and has deep knowledge and experience you can use in your cave city."

"Please tell her I am very busy and will not have time to see her. You and I have to get to the cave right now so it can be sealed," Howard replied. "We are the last to go."

"Mr. Blaine, she is extremely persistent and says you will be glad you talked to her," the secretary responded.

"Then please ask her to leave. Call a security bot if you have to. Then come back in here so we can make our escape."

The secretary left and then returned.

Howard continued, "There are secret underground tunnels below this building that double as a warehouse. We will go there now. It exits a mile away where a used attack helicopter I bought is waiting. There is a secret emergency cave entrance if we can get there before anyone discovers it. I invited two others to join us. I'll send the helicopter to pick them up as soon as it drops us off."

The secretary replied "What if those people out there see the helicopter? What if they find the other entrance?"

"Then we will be on our own. I instructed security to blow up the entrances and seal the cave if there was any danger a mob would break in. Let's go now."

The three of them walked to the elevator in a corner of his private office. He unlocked a secret panel and pressed the button for the underground tunnel.

*   *   *

Brandon Blaine was already in the main cave, overseeing final preparations, starting up the remaining equipment and systems, and waiting for his father and the other last-minute arrivals to enter through the secret access tunnel. As soon as everyone was accounted for, they would blow up all of the entrances, thus permanently sealing their fate and closing off all other options.

They checked the surveillance cameras and were immediately alarmed by what they saw! Half a dozen MSF27 advanced security robots were bringing power shovels and explosives to one of their cave entrances! The robots had already attacked and dispersed a mob that was trying to dog out the entrance. Now the MSF27s were attacking Blaine's less powerful SF10 security robots.

"What is going on? What can we do?" Brandon gasped.

One of his experts ventured a guess. "I think they've gone rogue. The MSF27s have a survival directive the SF10s lack. Their Achilles heel is their high power consumption. My guess is they're after our power plants, because generating stations above ground have mostly stopped working."

"How do we stop them? They are rational and they can make strategic plans. They are much more dangerous than any mob!"

"Our hope is that our SF10s can hold them off until their batteries go dead. The SF10s will sacrifice themselves if it gains them a tactical advantage. The MSF27s won't do that, in fact, for them it becomes every robot for itself. It's all about tactics and attrition now. If the MSF27s start to break through, we blow them up along with the cave entrance."

"How long do their batteries last?"

"I'm afraid I don't know that."

*   *   *

Elsewhere in another town, Larry Spelling looked excitedly forward to another marvelous day! Another overwhelming life-shaking experience! He adjusted his electronic internet and TV cap as he carefully placed it over the electrodes permanently implanted in his scalp.

There was a lot of claptrap about how children and adults alike spent so much time with the "tube" their minds would go to seed. But what was really happening? The smart ones were really the people who were absorbed by their electronic entertainment all day, enjoying themselves and enjoying life. These enlightened ones could experience a day at a tropical beach, a jungle safari, an exhilarating ski run, or absolutely anything they pleased via television, exactly as if they were there, without having to take any of the real physical risks of actually doing those things in person. Not only did you see and hear all the action, you could feel every sensation, experience every taste and smell, stir with every feeling.

When Larry watched a program about a safari or jungle trek, his muscles actually ached and he had callouses at the end of the day. If he watched a show with a beach scene, he would become sunburned. If there was a chase scene, he felt like he was actually driving the car. It all seemed so realistic, like you were actually there.

Meanwhile, the supposedly smart ones pointlessly tortured themselves with work, physical labor, scientific pursuits, and philosophical questions, most of which were no doubt pointless and unanswerable anyway. How could these misguided people be so crazy as to waste their lives in these kinds of painful pursuits, shunning all forms of real entertainment? They never experienced the virtual reality. At the end of their lives, how could they look back on things and accept that they never had any genuine enjoyment?

Virtual reality was so authentic Larry had even heard that sometimes, when people watched a movie about war, they could be crippled or dead by the end of the day, or if they watched scenes with people drinking at a bar, they became drunk themselves!

There was less drug use that way. VR was a cheaper and all-consuming experience, readily available, easy, and convenient.

Larry felt confused about what was actually real and what wasn't, but so what? It had crossed his mind that he might actually be doing something entirely different while he was absorbed in the virtual world. Maybe there were hackers breaking into the VR devices, people and politicians trying to control him, secretly discovering all his thoughts and actions unbeknownst to him. There was really no way to tell, and it didn't matter. Sometimes he had marks or bruises he couldn't explain. Well, why bother his mind with stupid thoughts. Who cares, anyway? Life is a happy VR episode each and every day.

Larry lay his aching, exhausted body down. After a day of action-adventure fare he was tired and would sleep well again that night. He carefully adjusted his head so the electrodes in his scalp wouldn't hurt him. Tomorrow would be another eventful, entertaining day, as always. Larry looked forward to whatever the VR producers would arrange for him.

There was all this groaning and moaning about some planet called "Invader." The VR people were telling him it was of no concern. At the same time, some of the televangelists were saying it was the end of civilization, that fire and brimstone followed by a frozen death was on the way, so better repent now! Well, even if it was, Larry knew what he would do about it. He would watch scenes on a tropical island, ocean waves crashing on the beaches, beautiful bikini-clad women everywhere. He would feel warm and tanned and happy. Right up until the moment he froze to death.

"Is everything ready? Time is up." Thor nervously wanted to know as his eyes glued themselves to the monitors. He had invested the best years of his life in this adventure but sadly, only future generations will know if he was successful.

"We're go. The launch window starts in about one hour. Final assembly of all twelve habitats was confirmed yesterday. The cryogenic modules are loaded and checked out, all robots re-initialized, final trajectory computations completed, inventories verified. They will launch at twenty-minute intervals once we are in suspended animation. Two advance probes and three laser/neutron weapon orbiters were launched a year ago. Last check all of them are on course and fully functional."

"It's a tight window. We need maximum slingshot from Invader and then from the sun. If we miss the window, we're screwed."

Everything was double and triple checked since there *was* no margin for error. The thermal nuclear boosters would fire first to leave orbit. They would fire again at each perigee along with the first stage fusion thermal rocket, and then fire again after each gravity slingshot. Then the boosters would be fired one last time until they were depleted, at which time they would be jettisoned and the magnetic sail deployed.

All the while, the spacecraft would be scooping in gas to use for fuel and reaction mass. When the plasma stream for the magnetic sail diminished, the sail would be retracted. and the first stage would resume firing until it was depleted and jettisoned. Next, the second stage would fire and be jettisoned when it was finished. Finally, the fusion ramjets would take over.

By this time, the spacecraft should be traveling fast enough for the interstellar ramjets to work with the new scoops. That is, the thrust would exceed the drag from the scoops. It's the same technique Titian used for the virus packages, and it worked flawlessly then. In the former case, they were able to achieve much more speed because of the much lighter virus payload. Slowing at the destination will primarily use the magnetic sail, with final slowing by small rocket. For the habitats, however, they also needed to use the ramjets with reverse thrust to help slow down the spacecraft initially, using residual hydrogen.

Thor couldn't help worrying. "Great! What about Conway?"

He had found help to dock and enter the on-orbit facility.

Michael broke the news. "He is still in the staging area. I had his cryogenic module relabeled 'Mountain Gorilla' and told payload control the latest trajectory calculations showed all twelve habitats were near overweight and they couldn't load the module. The timers are set to thaw him out starting in six hours, after all the launches are over. The recovery cycle is seventy-two hours, then he's on his own. He will blame you for everything."

Thor was relieved. "And for the first time ever he will be right. Hope that gives him some consolation. There is no more Titian. No board of directors, no corporate offices, no stock or ownership records, and no authority for Conway."

Thor was communicating from his home. He did not make the trip to the in-orbit facility. He decided to stay with Vanessa. Michael was in charge of the mission now.

"What will you do?" Michael radioed to Thor.

Thor answered, "Howard Blaine offered Vanessa and me a place in his cave. He is sending his helicopter this evening. I'll go there within the hour. Good luck, Michael."

Thor made a mental calculation about what the explorers could expect when they arrived at their new home. They will find a planet almost twice as far from its yellow type G2 yellow dwarf sun, the sun being just as bright as our familiar Gwydion, our type K2 orange dwarf star. The new sun will appear in the sky to be about nine-tenths the diameter of Gwydion. Solar tides on the new planet will only be about half as strong. A new earth year is about sixty-two percent longer than ours, three hundred sixty-five new earth days, with a day stretching about forty percent longer, and there is no comforting bright red jewel of a companion star to brighten the night.

An Astronomical Unit (AU) on the new planet will be nearly twice as large, as will a light year. So, new earth is nineteen-point-seven of its light years from us, and thirty-three additional new earth light years from the alternate new earth. The advance probes will arrive in one hundred eighty-eight new earth years if they survive the trip.

"We've only had twelve years (less than seven and a half new earth years) to pull this off and we did it! Relax and give yourself a well-deserved pat on the back!" Michael was proud.

By the time the astronauts arrive, their home planet, Gwydion Prime, will be two centuries into its deep freeze, its atmosphere frozen solid on its surface, an ember of inner warmth barely comforting it's deeply buried living remnant.

Thor looked up wistfully one last time, taking in the night sky, his last remaining opportunity to do so. The red dwarf Bethan, with its distant deep ruby red glow, was about to set in the west. Bethan was such a beautiful tiny pin-point jewel of a star, especially when it casts its red light at night, glowing brilliantly at a magnitude of negative seven. What a pity no planets orbit Bethan that could inhabited by higher life forms; they were all tidally locked and airless.

Thor wondered, what would it be like on the new planet? How would he have felt, an explorer on this dangerous new adventure? The same spirit that stirred his father possessed him for a moment. "Well," he consoled himself, "more than enough challenges lie ahead on Gwydion Prime. That's my adventure now."

Invader was just rising on the Eastern horizon, now four million miles away and consuming two and a half degrees of the sky, almost five times the diameter of Gwydion. Its once solid atmosphere was now boiling into a writhing mixture of hydrogen, helium, nitrogen, and carbon dioxide. It would make its closest approach in another five and a half days but already Gwydion was feeling its pull, accelerating spaceward, now eight million miles out from the orbit it had occupied for some eleven billion years now. At the same time, the air was growing ever colder.

Thor was quite sad he was not going on the mission and would never see the colonization of the new earth. At the same time, he was immensely pleased with his key role in bringing the mission about, and in the fact that his species, Galacticus magnificus, was about to take its first step toward mastering the galaxy, and indeed the universe.

It was time to accompany Vanessa to the cave before it was sealed off from the hordes who would be trying to break in. The government unions were joined by many others now, demanding that billionaires everywhere let their people into the caves. Within hours, it would be too late for that. Soon Invader would be close enough to raise monster tides and shore-destroying tsunamis, producing land tides that would set off volcanoes around the world while generating extra but temporary internal heat.

Vanessa put her arms around her husband, "I love you."

Thor responded, "I love you, too. Dress warm, my dearest."

Addendum 1
Characters

We each have our own experiences, knowledge, abilities, biases, blind spots, and points of view, so we all judge the people we meet differently. Therefore, the reader is encouraged to form his own opinion of the characters presented.

1. The People

Each personality is said to be a coherent system, like an ecosystem, that seeks its own equilibrium. Whenever there is a disturbance, it is said that the system will try to return to its equilibrium point unless the disturbance is so great the entire system irreparably fails. So then, what is the equilibrium point for each character?

<u>Thor Haierdood, Jr.</u>: Thor is absorbed in his work. Too much so; it is his main passion in life. He is ambitious in that he seeks ever larger and more challenging technical challenges. He wants to be validated by receiving the same recognition as his famous father. He is aware of his coworkers and knows he needs them to accomplish his goals. Therefore, he is studious about steering their work, pushing them to develop their skills, and rewarding them when they come through for him. As a result, most of his subordinates are quite loyal to him and willing to work hard. Thor focuses on problems to be solved and is not interested in casting blame. He is not very socially aware, and at first does not really understand his wife's emphasis on their personal relationship. He accepts prevailing social conventions at face value and without question at an unconscious level. Such matters are simply not in his field of view. He is extremely proud of his species and its accomplishments. This pride contributes to his ego. He implicitly accepts the popular view that the species and its society were nearly perfected through its almost godlike response to a series of historical trials. It is therefore an obvious logical imperative that the

species and culture be preserved. For Myers-Briggs fans, Thor is an ENTP.

Michael: Michael values loyalty, trust, faithfulness, honor, dedication, and hard work. Subconsciously Thor "bought" his devotion when he brought Michael from their previous company, promoted him, and gave him more responsibility. He is detail oriented and organized. Michael is unaware he is caught in a pleasant trap. He is an ISTJ.

Annie Kolar: Annie wants immediate gratification and the more the better. She is driven by whatever impulse pops up from her unconscious and possesses her mind at the moment. Her thought and values are determined by her wants, and she tends to be obsessive about them. To Annie, people are no more than cardboard cutouts that can either dispense things she wants or get in her way, or sometimes a mixture of the two. She is not consciously aware of any of this. She has a number of favored means to get what she wants. First choice is by manipulation, bullying, intimidation, and invective. Guilt is her ally. This provides an ample excuse to pour out endless streams of venom on those who richly deserve it. If this tactic fails, she will try to seduce or manipulate with gossip. Annie views herself as a dispenser of truth, logic, and common sense. She knows better than anyone else. If there is something she doesn't know, it is because it is trivial or stupid and not worth bothering about. The best way with people is to be up front and confront them with the truth of their inadequacies. If you don't agree with her wisdom, or fail to provide what she wants, or you get in her way or inconvenience her, you invite endless wrath and abuse, and deservedly so. Annie's wants determine her values which in turn determine her beliefs. All external inputs are either filtered, revised and rewritten, or excluded entirely so they become consistent her beliefs and wants. Some would claim that deep down inside, she knows something is wrong, but that is simply not the case. Nothing that contradicts her outlook gets into her head in the first place, so there are no doubts. Her wants spring unconsciously from the wants of the moment and are therefore inevitably contradictory. But since just one or only a few impulses possess her mind at any one time, the conflict is averted. Annie craves control over people, acknowledgement, the freedom to do whatever she wants with impunity, and more than ample means to never have to worry about it. While Annie has the gift of unconscious radar that homes in on others' weaknesses and exploits them without mercy, a trait that serves her well, she has a secret vulnerability herself. In the past everyone has eventually abandoned her (run away in most cases). She has experienced no long-term loyalty. She is needy but conceals it with an appearance of strength. Annie is driven by her shadow, with little conscious awareness or control. It is always the case that when shadow takes over the mind, everything is projected. This means anyone who knows what to look for and can remain detached enough (not an easy thing) can see through her, while at the same time she is blind to it all herself. Eventually, those around her either flee if they can or try to wall her off. For Myers-Briggs fans she is an ESFJ.

Bernie M. Conway: Like Annie Kolar, Conway is ruled by his shadow, but he craves power along with its representative and first cousin, money. He will use any means and anyone to get what he wants. However, Conway is subtle, nuanced, and detached enough to strategize and exert a cynical control. He is not always a captive of the moment. He possesses an overactive pair of alpha male genes. Anyone else in a position to make decisions or who has any authority is a potential rival and obstacle, and he is always looking for a vulnerability to use to eliminate this competition and seize their sphere of influence for himself, when the opportunity arises. He searches for others' vulnerabilities, always looking for weapons to sink them with. He is afraid there are others out there like him and he could become a target, in fact, so as far as he knows everyone is dangerous until proven otherwise. He himself is a shifting target, hard to pin down, revealing nothing that can be used against him. Nobody knows what he really thinks or what his real plan is. He treats his bosses and equals differently than his subordinates. For the former, flattery is his favorite tactic and he is a master con, while at the same time badmouthing them by innuendo behind their backs. To subordinates, he is a dictator, and no demand is over the top. He takes credit with his bosses for anyone else's successes he can get away with, at the same time publicizing their real or (most often) trumped up failures. Divide and conquer is his motto. He embellishes his claimed accomplishments and talents endlessly. Conway is well aware that he has never made a mistake in his life, and that everything that has ever gone wrong is the result of someone else's stupidity. For Myers-Briggs fans he is an ESTJ.

<u>Brandon Cathcart and Joseph Huber</u>: Like Conway, Brandon Cathcart and Joseph Huber are career politicians and have nearly the same personality. Absolute power is their holy grail. They are convinced that everyone around them has a hidden agenda and after all, you can never tell if someone is secretly plotting to do *them* in. "Pre-emptive strike" is their middle name. Both are ISTJ, though they can fake being an E. That is, they play their cards close to the vest but can pretend to be your friend and confidant (revealing strategic lies dressed up like truths) if it suits their purpose.

<u>Reverend Franklin</u>: Rev. Franklin is a heroic and unifying figure. He represents, and to an extent is possessed by, the Self. People, their feelings, and their problems are real to Rev. Franklin and he sincerely wants the best for everyone, which to him means unification (melding) with his version of the Holy One and its attendant belief system. This vision and sincerity hold great attraction for many and Rev. Franklin has a large flock of followers. His fame and influence can be used by others for their purposes just as the legacy of Martin Luther King is used by a few politicians to further their own ambitions. Rev. Franklin could turn the tables and in turn use the politicos' power to increase his own following and influence, but to do this consciously would be hypocritical, cynical, and ultimately self-defeating. That operation must be carried out by the unconscious shadow or by the street-wise Peters unbeknownst to Rev. Franklin. If Rev. Franklin knew about such machinations, it would threaten his inner unity. Thus, he can remain pure, and avoid becoming defiled. Rev. Franklin's first inclination is to galvanize his followers to prayer and repentance, to accept the Holy Plan for them. However, others with ulterior motives can help Rev. Franklin to expand his influence and distribute his life-saving message throughout the galaxy and for all time, creating an excruciating but unconscious dilemma. Like Annie

Kolar, whatever happens to or around Rev. Franklin is interpreted and filtered in a manner consistent with his firm beliefs. Unlike Annie, those beliefs are more-or-less self-consistent and not changeable based on momentary impulses. Thus, there is an internal consistency and harmony that is completely lacking in a narcissistic type. For Myers-Briggs fans, Rev. Franklin is an NFP and a conduit from I to E.

Rock Peters: A trickster, he unconsciously knows Rev. Franklin is dedicated to his message and beliefs, and he therefore seems like an odd couple partner to Rev. Franklin. Peters can transform idealistic inner images into real-world action. The consequences are far-reaching at times, but Peters himself remains steadfastly faithful to Rev. Franklin's message. For Myers-Briggs fans, Peters is ESFP.

Vanessa Haierdood: She is a creature of simple devotion, but she doesn't understand Thor's work or purpose. She is needy and just wants someone strong to be with her who she can completely absorb herself into. This is not a great fit with Thor, but she offers him support when nobody else does and she has a definite attraction for him.

Howard Blaine: Howard Blaine, founder of Blaine Industries, is a self-made billionaire. He had planned to pass his business down to his son Brandon, but instead, his son's legacy will be a well-appointed cave. At least, both of them have always enjoyed caving in their spare time. Blaine has definite goals and ambitions but views his purpose as providing goods and services to those who need them, and profiting in the process. He is not a ruthless competitor, and has a degree of compassion for his employees. However, because of his single-minded focus, his conception of other people is somewhat abstract, and he sometimes inadvertently steps on them. Blaine is a global, high level, systematic thinker and an eternal optimist. He is sure there is a way to overcome any obstacle. Brandon is a chip off the old block and his father's right-hand man. However, Brandon has never had to struggle or take big chances like his father, and tends to be much more careful and conservative. Therein lies the central developing conflict between the two of them that both want to avoid. Myers-Briggs type INTP (Howard) and ENTP (Brandon).

<u>Maynard Kolar</u>: Maynard is a well-known and often quoted economist. He views not only his subject matter of economics, but all of his surroundings and his life as the predictable outcome of a set of econometric models. Therefore, he has absolutely no grounding in common sense or real-life experiences, and had no idea what he was getting into when he married Annie. Maynard is an example of someone whose equilibrium was shattered, and he was propelled into a new and very different state of mind.

<u>Chipper, Jenna, Theo, and Leah Hurlock</u>: The Hurlock family are decent, hardworking, and responsible people. They have a simple and comforting view of life. The parents have transmitted solid values to their inquisitive and studious children. They endure discrimination against their social group with dignity and good spirit. Like all Canaille, they are naturally dependent and susceptible to charismatic, dominant individuals. At the same time, they, like all Canaille, are fully aware of the genetic trick that was played on them and are angry, hurt, and distrustful of authority figures and their hidden agendas. For the parents, this anger is mostly buried. They are aware of what happened to their class at both a conscious and unconscious level. This contradiction makes for much anxiety, especially for those who have not reached a compromise with it. Like a majority of Canaille, the Hurlocks are highly attracted to, and loyal followers of, the Reverend Franklin and his spiritual message, even though he is not one of them himself. Many of their values come from the Reverend's teachings. Chipper Hurlock is Myers-Briggs type ESFJ. Jenna Hurlock is type ESFP.

<u>Zerathud</u>: Zerathud has always been depressed and narcissistic. His motivation and ambition are MIA. He likes his well-paid do-nothing (or at least very little) job, where he doesn't have to challenge or exert himself much, since doing so would bring up issues he would rather not face. He has been a secret (now not so secret) alcoholic since he was old enough to steal from his parents' liquor cabinet without getting caught. He tends to be a loner, but occasionally it's nice to have an agreeable drinking buddy to validate his habits. He himself becomes

more agreeable and malleable when he drinks. For Myers-Briggs fans he is an ISFP.

Fiona Facre: Fiona is a strictly by-the-book no nonsense individual, and nobody gets around her, or so it seems. Underneath she is insecure with little self-esteem, and prone to depression and feelings of desperation. Enforcing the rules gives her a sense of purpose, a way to dedicate and organize herself. If someone comes along to flatter her, pat her on the back, take her seriously, take her onto their confidence, she will crumble and find a way to bend her rules. Manipulative types could be her downfall if she is unlucky, and she will never be able to see through them in advance. Fiona is Myers Briggs type ISFJ.

David James: James is a totally narcissistic and self-absorbed introvert. He believes his fantasies are real. At the same time, he has a sixth sense about what other people are missing in life, what their urgent and unfulfilled needs are. And, he knows how to spin his fantasy so it appears to others to fill those holes. This gives him great charisma and allows him to be a master manipulator. In a somewhat healthier life, he would be the one who sold the refrigerators to the Eskimos and laughed about it. James is a power-hungry authoritarian and demands absolute obedience. He demands that his followers validate his every fantasy. Transgressors are treated in the harshest of terms. He also demands that his followers actively separate themselves from former friends and family, and discourages them from thinking (he will tell them what to think). Followers are taught to be suspicious of and, indeed, hate, outsiders. Everyone, followers and outsiders alike, are judged on the basis of how well they satisfy James' dictates and wants. All of this makes his followers highly dependent on him. Of course, with few reality checks, his mental illness was bound to progress. Over time he becomes more sadistic, ever more judgmental, and assumes an even greater cloak of superiority and power. James is Myers-Briggs type ISFJ.

Norman Carson: Thor views Dr. Norman Carson as a no-nonsense potential leader of the astronaut group. He seems to be a natural leader and has most of the qualities mentioned. The others tend to look to him for an opinion. His Myers-Briggs type is ENTJ. Myers-

Briggs types for some of the other astronauts are John Forbes (ESTP), Evelyn Wallace (ISTP), Charles Wallace (ISFJ), Renee Jenner (ESTJ), Peter Skinner (ISTJ), Elizabeth Osler (ESTP), and Van Newman (INTP).

<u>Warner Titian</u>: The long-deceased founder of Titian Space systems traced his lineage to the fifteenth-century Italian artist Titian (Tiziano) who was called "The Sun Amidst Small Stars" by his contemporaries. "Titian" became an orange-red color reminiscent of a late K dwarf star.

Note on the Myers-Briggs:

The Myers-Briggs classifications originated when psychologist Carl Jung asked himself why his viewpoint differed so markedly from that of his mentor Sigmund Freud. It describes a person's approach to life based on four classification pairs (three invented by Jung plus one added by Myers and Briggs). There are no judgments or standards associated with these categories; they are purely descriptive. There are degrees, that is, someone can be either extreme or anywhere in the middle for each of the pairs. What follows is a very much simplified version.

First, one can be introverted or extraverted. As originally defined, this describes whether one's motivation comes from internal standards (I) or from the praise, standards, encouragement, or discouragement of others (E).

Second, one can be a big idea person (intuitive or N) or a detail person (sensory or S), that is, do you first notice the forest (N) or the trees (S). Now right off you can see that the philosophical type tends to be IN whereas the man of action will tend toward ES, but there are no hard and fast rules.

Third, one can make decisions and judgments by thinking (T) or feeling (F). Thinking generally means decisions are made on the basis of logical principles or assumptions. Feeling means decisions are based on emotions and feelings, which could be your own feelings or that of others.

Fourth, one can be judgmental (J) or perceiving (P). Type A personalities tend to be J while easy going types who take things as they come and don't ask a lot of questions tend to be P, but this is not absolute. If one is J, the F-T pair predominates whereas for a P the N-S pair predominates. Myers and Briggs added P and J to Jung's original three pairs.

Obviously, there are varying degrees and combinations for all of the pairs. It is also debatable whether one's classification is variable depending on the situation and stage of life, though certainly everyone has a comfortable base state.

Myers and Briggs came up with a test to determine one's classification.

2. The Robots

Tax5: Tax5 is the fourth revision of the original Tax1 tax collecting robot. Tax1 turned out to be a little too simple. It was specified by the government to have a single goal of maximizing the amount (Net Present Value) of money and property collected. It was equipped with a baseball bat and a sensor to recognize knee-caps. The latest Tax5 models have infrared, motion, x-ray, sonic and every other conceivable sensor along with laser and neutron weapons. They even come with two full days of political speech re-runs to soften up really tough cases. The Tax2, 3, 4, and 5 had full language capability. The Myers-Briggs robot type is HRM5.

AI74B Master Intelligence: Designed for maximum intelligence and speed, with adjustable heuristics, it has a rudimentary model of psychology that attempts to understand why people say what they do. A persistent problem has been that people can't recognize when the robot is playing or practicing to hone its skills, although other robots can always tell. Like most AI robots, it also has language capability. The Myers-Briggs robot type is FAS1.

SF10 Security Robot: The SF10 is big, powerful, and intimidating. It recognizes people, weapons, drones, other robots, and territorial boundaries. In particular, it is trained to recognize a ranked hierarchy of corporate and individual owners, and can only be directed by these entities. It is somewhat intelligent and tries to infer a plan and purpose behind what it perceives. However, it has difficulty inferring the motives behind other robots' actions. It also has language capability and can read between the lines. SF10s are usually purchased as a force battalion, and individual SF10s recognize, and exchange new information and skills they learn with other SF10s in their battalion. Thus, they can coordinate their actions. The SF10's directives are simple: to protect the life and property of explicitly identified companies or individuals within certain boundaries, to prevent unauthorized entry to designated places, and to prevent taking of their owner's property without official digital permission, with exceptions authorizable digitally by designated individuals. Other robots, whether corporate, personal, or government controlled, are always considered potential adversaries. They are also trained to resist hacking. SF10s will sacrifice themselves strategically to meet these objectives. The Myers-Briggs robot type is FRM4.

MSF27 Security Robot: The MSF27 is a more sophisticated, more formidable, major upgrade to the simplistic SF10. It includes a survival directive (instinct) which the SF10 lacks. They can coordinate with drones, equipment, active sensors and cameras, and staff, monitor broadcasts and scanners, and negotiate with police, government, and other robots. They were only available during the year prior to the catastrophe. They are more powerful than the old SF10s, but the increased formidability and computing capability comes at the cost of a much higher power consumption and the necessity for frequent recharging. The Myers-Briggs robot type is FRM3.

TH22 Infantry Robot: This robot is designed to defend and seize ground, to recognize many kinds of threats, to infer the plan and intentions of enemy robots, weapons, and military personnel. It normally operates under the direction of a GH50 series master tactical and strategic computer. It is aware of, and coordinates its activities with, other TH22s. However, it can operate independently of other robots if communications are cut. The TH22 can be fitted with a large variety of weapons. It can also operate over many different kinds of terrain. It does not have language capability. Some versions incorporate jet packs. The Myers-Briggs robot type is HRM3.

EHB4 Hackbot: The EHB4 attempts to hack other robots. Its directives are selectable, that is, it can seek to disable target robots by altering or deleting critical directives, schemas, or primitives; or it can turn another robot against its owners by changing its directives and loading the target with the new percepts, schemas, goals and subgoals, concepts, and models to carry out this sabotage; or it can read and reconstruct an opposing robot's memory and communications to obtain intelligence information. The hackbot must first tap into the robot's memory and into other robot communications by doing a "robot mind probe" so it can reconstruct how the robot works. Naturally, hackbots are quite complex and need huge fast memory, have super-computer capabilities, have elaborate sensors, and consume a lot of power. Usually, they must be mobile and try to station themselves near their intended targets. Mobile hackbots consume their batteries quickly, and since they are large, they cannot easily hide. To solve these problems, they are sometimes stationary and plugged into permanent power, while relying on smaller, less capable, but longer-lasting EHB2M mobile assistant hackbots to pursue their prey for them. Opposing hackbots sometimes attempt to hack each other.

Dr. Hydroxide: This was the robot version of a patchwork quilt, assembled from odds and ends.

3. The Mobs

Impending disaster, defeat, frustration, social violence and disorder, controlled regimentation, resented forced obedience, all wear on a population and ingrain themselves throughout their conscious and unconscious thought. Populations become attracted to a coalescing widespread archetypal image, a vision that frees them from their common predicament. When such common images form simultaneously in a group of people, they become unknowingly focused and expectant. They are ripe for a psychological takeover.

If water is quickly super-cooled to below freezing it remains a liquid. As soon as a single tiny ice crystal forms the entire container will suddenly and simultaneously freeze over. In exactly the same way, the mass psyche primed with an archetypal image is ready to suddenly coalesce into a mob driven by an irresistible force from within. The precipitating particle will be the most volatile and archetypally possessed among them who suddenly trips over the edge into driven, uncontrolled action. The crowd instantly and instinctively follows. Or, the precipitating particle could be a cynical demagogue who senses the potential of the primed and expectant crowd; he has one foot and one eye in with the crowd himself but the other eye is focused on his own agenda, and he instinctively senses the possibility to focus the crowd as a tool to further his aims.

Mobs are a direct conduit from the unconscious to group action. They entirely bypass conscious filtering. Mobs are like dreams, or in many cases, nightmares, except that unlike dreams, real action is not inhibited.

Unlike bureaucracies and institutions, mobs have no accreted baggage, no added personal agendas, and no fossilized formats. They are a pure form.

The liquor rebellion: There are few problems in life so severe they won't succumb to a sufficient dose of alcohol. But the alcohol had run out while the problems continued to intensify. Limitless liquor was the answer! Just help yourself and life can be perfect.

Food riot mobs: Driven by hunger and cold, resentful that the well connected, wealthy, or other privileged groups have plenty while they, the deserving, suffer. Revenge (viewed as justice) and food are part of their vision.

<u>Canaille mobs</u>: Some people just had enough. They were tired of trying to cope when nothing worked. The few rich and well-connected were fine while everyone else suffered grievously. There was no hope. People were so angry they couldn't contain it anymore and it just poured out. They didn't just want to vent their anger and frustration. They wanted revenge, to make everyone else have a turn to find out what it was like with no food. Take from the fat cats and let them suffer for a change. The Canaille were quick to express repressed anger and they were looking for a movement to coalesce around, but unorganized and lacking in initiative themselves. Unconscious instincts said their community was the place to start a mob and then spread it to the other cities. Images of blind revenge, rage, and looting for free valuables in order to get even helped to focus these mobs.

Addendum 2
Elements

1. Plot Elements

Considering the many common hazards lurking in the galaxy and the billions of years in the lifetime of the average star, sudden unexpected life-exterminating events should be expected. How can an intelligent race respond if they have enough warning for such an event?

Four possibilities are presented here: passive introverted (pray and make peace with God, prepare for the next life), passive extroverted (live it up like there is no tomorrow because there probably isn't), active introverted (build a refuge and hunker down, prolonging life as long as possible), and active extroverted (identify and migrate to other planets, preserve the species and its culture if possible, and in spite of the fact that it might unexpectedly mean replacing an existing biological culture). Not only is there no preferred resolution, but the choice evolves into a moral and spiritual dilemma. What, therefore, is the best course of action? The characters in the story are compelled by their character, culture, history, and beliefs to choose a particular path and they have no real conscious choice in the matter.

There is a fifth possibility: denial. However, reality has a way of imposing itself and forcing a choice sooner or later.

2. Hazards

The universe is a shooting gallery, full of hazards. Rogue planets, small black holes, brown dwarfs, and other bodies wander around unseen. Stars can wander through relatively dense clouds of gas or cosmic nurseries, expanding clouds of gas and radiation from novae, gamma ray bursts, near the jets of neutron stars and magnetars, near the radiation-filled galactic center where radiation from star bursts will sooner or later sterilize every planet, and near other intense radiation hazards. There is always the possibility of wandering too close to an exploding supernova, though this is a fairly rare event. Most ordinary stars form planets and have an Oort cloud of debris extending out up to around a light year or more. Passing stars or other massive objects pass through the Oort cloud from time to time, dislodging meteors and comets that come crashing into the inner solar system. Giant planets may or may not be found approximately where they formed, or in inner solar systems where they are called "hot Jupiters", or out in the Oort cloud to stir things up. Planetary orbits tend to circularity in the plane of their star's rotation, but can also be highly elliptical or inclined. It is quite common for planets to be thrown into interplanetary space, condemned to wander the icy reaches of space for eternity, occasionally wandering through an Oort cloud or even into an inner solar system. It is estimated that our galaxy may contain hundreds of billions up to a few trillion of such rogue planets ranging from less than earth sized to 10 or 20 Jupiter masses. Often these are dislodged by hot Jupiters migrating inward, or by Neptune-sized planets thrown about by super Jupiters. Planets ranging from Neptune-sized to 10 or more Jupiter masses can be found in orbits anywhere from very close to their parent star to within the Oort cloud, in orbits ranging from circular to highly elliptical. In some systems a 1 to 10 Jupiter mass planet can lurk in the Oort cloud, having been displaced from a closer-in orbit.

There are trillions of bullets in the galactic firing range, nudged towards potential targets by long range gravity.

3. Robotic Life and Robotic Forced Evolution

Gene-culture coevolution refers to the influence of culture on the evolution of human traits and vice-versa. When artificial intelligence progresses to the point where it outstrips human action and thinking capabilities, and where it alters and drives cultural thought, we will arrive at gene-computer coevolution. This is one of the factors Thor was thinking of that "purified and perfected" the species in his view. Since there is a limit to brain capacity due to the high energy consumption of the brain and the ability to satisfy these energy

Page 196

requirements, what direction will robot evolution take when robots have the ability to re-program themselves?

4. Archetypes on Other Planets

Any particular planet will have its unique climate, gravity, atmospheric pressure and composition, climatic and evolutionary history, physiological possibilities, level of tectonic activity, frequency of evolution altering catastrophes, predatory and symbiotic possibilities, metallic abundance, core size and magnetic field, rotation rate, presence or absence of stabilizing moons or planets or companion stars, level of host star activity and hazards, galactic environment, particularly adaptive skills, adaptations, and temperaments, and so on. The resulting physical forms, hereditary mechanisms, and behavior will vary markedly as a result. One could even come up with a matrix of tables conjecturing a range of possible conditions and the resulting possible physical forms and archetypal behaviors that might evolve in response.

Even supposing theoretically identical planets, the results of evolution could be wildly different, as can the ultimate planetary environment.

Extinction level events could result in stagnant life forms, for example, if an asteroid hadn't wiped out the dinosaurs and it was still an age of reptiles; or the converse, two or more extinction events in quick succession nearly wiping out life, resulting in a restart from different initial conditions.

Close passing stars may stir up the Oort cloud at random, unpredictable times.

Path-dependent evolution will constrain what can evolve, that is, new structures are often built from or on top of existing forms, so that possibilities for future evolution are dependent on what came before.

The proportion of land and ocean, and the size of islands and continents, along with the degree of isolation of different populations is another factor. Metallicity will be different, resulting in variations in

Page 197

tectonic activity and in magnetic shielding from solar radiation. Solar type, flare and other activity, year and day and axial tilt variations, orbital eccentricity and the make-up and distribution and influence of giant planets will be different. The wavelength of peak solar radiation will vary, affecting photosynthesis or even making this impossible. Insufficient photosynthesis may prevent formation of an ozone layer, resulting in too much mutation inducing ultraviolet. The list goes on and on, so that, even if life is commonplace, twin Earths might be scarce. Hence the need for extensive terraforming that occurs over a long timeframe before colonization can occur.

All of this has been ignored here to make the story more accessible.